PROJECT CHARON 1: RE-ENTRY

A SPACE OPERA ADVENTURE

PATTY JANSEN

DID YOU KNOW?

Project Charon 1: Re-entry is also available in audio. Visit https://pattyjansen.com to find out more.

GET FREE EBOOKS

Visit pattyjansen.com
to sign up for Patty's mailing list. You get four series starter
ebooks for free!

CHAPTER ONE

TINA WAS DOING the books when the doorbell to the shop rang.

The old-fashioned tinkle was music to her ears. It meant customers, and there were never quite enough of those.

She gladly abandoned her tangled finances, shoving the computer in the drawer with the bookkeeping module still on the screen.

The man who came in, tall and broad shouldered, was not a local but he looked vaguely familiar to her. It wasn't unusual for strangers to come into the shop, even if it was located twenty minutes out of Gandama and only thirty people lived in the remote hamlet of Dickson's Creek.

People around here went to all kinds of lengths to live their lives out of the neighbours' view. It wouldn't be the first time that someone had moved in with family or married a local, or someone had died and the house had been sold and the community only found out months later.

That was how people rolled around here.

She couldn't see his face because he was backlit by the light that streamed in from the window. It was late afternoon and the desert sun was coming in straight from over the dusty fields where the neighbour's farm robot moved backwards and forwards, raking rocks out of the soil.

The stranger wound his way between the shelves and tables displaying electronics and security equipment without stopping to look at any of it.

Tina made herself look taller behind the counter of the shop. She quickly rearranged a box of the latest sensors that she had obtained from a dealer in Peris City last week, hoping he would buy a handful of them. Someone had done that just this morning. Like everything that came from off world, they weren't cheap.

The man came up to the shop counter and placed both his hands on the surface.

Strange hands they were, too. His fingers were stubby and very short. The skin was mottled and his fingers were covered with little elongated flaps of skin, like warts. He had so many of them that he looked like a toad.

His nails had grown in a curved fashion, like the claws of an animal. He had filed the ends into points.

He wore a long-sleeved jacket despite the heat. The top of the zip fastening was open, revealing a glimmer of body armour. Around his waist he wore a belt with large metal eyelets—a pirate belt. Typically, members of the pirate—or Freeranger—gangs wore one of these, usually with an array of weapons dangling from it.

Those belts had become fashionable in Peris City recently, but it still made Tina do a double take when she saw one.

"How can I help you?" she asked, her heart still thudding.

She reached under the counter for the fence post she kept there as a weapon, although it would do little against high-quality armour like that, if thuggery was the purpose of his visit. And she wasn't sure. He looked too clean and civilised for that.

"I'm here for the loan," the man said.

His voice was deep and gravelly, but again, she sensed she'd heard it before. His face, equally covered in warts, was utterly strange to her. The only part of him that didn't make Tina's skin crawl was his eyes. They were brown and clear.

"I haven't applied for a loan," Tina said. Since when did lenders send people who dressed like pirates, no matter how fashionable the attire?

"It's not about me giving out more money. It's about getting my money back."

"I don't understand. Who are you? I don't owe you any money."

"You don't have a loan for this shop?"

"Why should that be any of your business? I don't even know who you are."

"I'm Simon Fosnet. I asked you, do you have a loan?"

"I do, but I have never missed any payments." Because getting tangled up with unscrupulous lenders was one of the ways people got themselves into trouble in Gandama.

"That's right. I need the money."

And it was only at this point that she figured out who he was.

When she had started the shop, Tina had borrowed money to buy the premises off one of the town's loan brokers. The money came from a rich citizen of Gandama.

She had met the man a few times, but he had later moved to Peris City, leaving the administration of the loan to a broker. For years she had made regular payments.

Was this really the same man?

She couldn't clearly remember what he had looked like back then, but she would have remembered if he had all those strange warts on his face. What sort of horrible condition was this?

She stammered, "I'm sorry. I didn't recognise you."

And, looking at his face, she *still* didn't recognise him, his disfigurement was that bad. But now that she thought of it, she did recognise his name.

He snorted, but didn't comment on it. "Yes. It's unusual for the lender to ask for a return of the funds, but I have a situation where I need the money quickly. It's medical, you must understand."

"Yes, I understand." Shudder. Whatever was wrong with him?

"Good, then I want the entire amount repaid in full within three days."

"Sorry—I didn't hear you properly. Did you say three days?"

"That's what I said."

"But wait. Where am I going to find that kind of money within three days?" Tina's heart was hammering. Three days was ridiculous. "Can't you give me a bit longer? Nothing in Gandama moves fast."

"I'm afraid that's not my problem. I simply need the money fast. You can find a loan broker to get you a different loan from someone else."

Yes, but who else would lend her the money? Gandama was doing badly enough. All the people who used to have successful businesses had left in the last few years. With all the unsavoury business and thuggery that was going on, the only business that was still close to making a profit was that of selling security equipment. And that business was hers.

Then he added, "There is another solution."

"Is there?"

Any solution that didn't involve the rendering of certain "services", for which she was too old anyway. Surely they couldn't be that desperate?

"You could give me that collection of yours in your backyard."

What the...? "My cactuses?"

"Yes."

A cold hand of fear clamped around her heart. No way would she give him her cactuses. She had invested far too much time and research in them. Without them, she couldn't survive. They were part of her business, and to sell him her breeding stock... just no. She had taken years to develop them, initially because she liked them, and they liked being around her. But then people in Peris City had become interested in them, *collectors* of cactuses, who paid lots of money for the very special ones she developed.

"Yes, it's easy. I take the collection, and you keep the money."

"All of the money?" That sounded too good to be believed. In fact, she didn't believe it. This had to be some sort of trap.

"Yes."

"Would you sign for that?"

He snorted. "What do you expect? No, this is a deal I can only offer to you in person, and only because I'm partial to cactuses."

"They're for yourself?" If she weren't already dubious about this "deal", then she would be now. There was no reason for him to want the cactuses, if he needed money, as he said earlier. Medical treatment *had* to be more important than cactuses, no matter how much they were worth. No matter how much rich people were trying to park money in assets that had no value on paper, but could easily be sold on the black market.

And if she agreed, what would happen to her loan if he wouldn't sign a written deal?

It would take her far too long to build up breeding stock of a similar quality, by which time the cactus craze in Peris City would have worn off, leaving her with a big hole in her budget, if she could even survive that long.

Oh no, other than the fact that she didn't want to sell the cactuses, Tina didn't trust this at all. What was up with him anyway? Why did he have all those disgusting warts on his face and hands?

"Can I think about this?" Anything but that. She'd have to find some other way of getting him the money.

"I still need the money within three days."

"I understand. But I still want to think about it. I'll get you the money as soon as I can."

He held up three warted, curve-nailed fingers before her face. "Three days."

"I will try."

"Not try. I need the money. Or I will use more convincing methods."

And as abruptly as he had come, he left the shop again. The bell above the door tinkled when he left. There was nothing cheerful about it this time.

Tina let her shoulders slump. Where the hell would she get that much money within three days?

"Who was that?" said a young male voice at the back of the shop. Tina still had to get used to the dark tone it had taken on a few weeks ago.

The voice was accompanied by whirring and clicking as Rex wheeled his armour away from the work bench where he had been fixing equipment and lumbered to the door, the armour going zzzz-click-zzzzz-click with each step.

"Just a customer," Tina said. The shop was her business. Rex was too young to have to deal with the trouble of running it.

"That didn't sound like just a customer to me. It sounded like he was going to be difficult."

Rex was also getting smart. "Don't worry about it," Tina said.

"Did you know him?"

"Not really."

"Then what did he want?"

"Just shop business. Why are you asking?" Seriously, what was it with all the questions? Rex rarely said boo.

"Old Janusz told me yesterday to watch out because he's seen a lot of weird characters around recently. Pirates and those."

Tina thought of the pirate belt the man had been wearing. But it had been far too new for it to belong to a real Freeranger pirate. They had become fashion items. Everyone wore them.

"Where does Janusz see these pirates anyway? He sits on his back veranda all day playing with his farming robots. He doesn't go anywhere, except when he needs to complain about something."

Rex shrugged, which made his harness wobble. "I'm just repeating what he said."

But a faint feeling of unease came over her. Tina had heard the rumours about the pirates as well.

Pirates was a loose term for those people who rejected Federacy rule as a form of dictatorship. Space was meant to be free for all.

Not all of them had criminal intentions, but they often resorted to crimes, because, even the principled ones still needed to live, and they were ineligible for Federacy support.

Some people, like Janusz, got their definition of pirates mixed up. The real Freerangers were in space, and wouldn't come down to planets. Janusz's "pirates" were just petty criminals.

"Don't worry about pirates. The man came from Peris City. He's not a pirate."

"Are you sure? Janusz said that some of them were getting bold and were going into shops."

"Yes, I'm sure. I don't know this customer well, but I know *of* him. He's not a pirate. And old Janusz says a lot of things. Most of them are in his head. Don't let him upset you with all these things. They're mostly heavily embellished gossip."

He snorted. "How else am I supposed to find out what's going on? You never tell me anything."

"That's because the things he says are all nonsense."

"Then tell me the truth according to Dr Tina Freeman." He put on a self-important voice when he said that. "I'm fifteen. I can handle it."

Tina lifted her hands, breathed in deeply, her mind full of reasons why there was no single truth and about how

people in power made you see what they wanted you to see
—but it was all unimportant.

So she let out her breath again.

Money. Getting another loan. Those were the important
things. She didn't have time for yet another argument with
her son. There had been far too many of them already.

CHAPTER TWO

IT WAS afternoon and too late for Tina to go into town to find anyone who might be able to lend her money. The offices would still be open by the time she made the twenty-minute drive there, but these types of people wouldn't see her without an appointment, and it would take too long to arrange one. Because in Gandama one did not make any unannounced visits to financial people. They might think you'd come to rob them.

She would have to go tomorrow morning, and a feeling of panic clamped around her heart. That was one day of the three she had to raise the money.

Three days—it was ridiculous. And did he really suggest he was going to use threats to get his money if she didn't comply? What would that achieve? She couldn't make any money where there wasn't any.

She opened the drawer and took out the computer that still displayed the financial program. Tina had written it herself, and it plotted out in detail how much money she needed to earn to pay off enough of her loan by the time Rex was twenty-one to give him a comfortable life. She would give him the shop, the house and the little sanctuary she had built for him.

But this ridiculous request upset everything.

Her shop account held enough to pay her bills, her suppliers and her regular loan repayment. Her personal accounts held enough money to survive, a bit extra to pay for any unforeseen doctor visits or repairs.

But the column labelled "Debts and assets" was still in the red to the extent of ninety-seven thousand credits, the outstanding debt on the shop and the land.

Where in the world would she raise that much in this little time?

Unless—no, she would have to leave the shop and she couldn't do that. And it wouldn't be possible within three days anyway.

She shoved the computer back into the drawer. If she wasn't successful, then there was no point in doing these books. She would have to sell the shop, and abandon all the work she had put into making it a place where Rex could move around freely.

She abandoned any attempt at the accounts, and went out the back to the yard.

At this time of the day, the sun was behind the house, creating an area of shade at the bottom of the steps. The air was still searing hot, exuding the omnipresent smell of hot dust that one only noticed when it was missing.

In a previous life, the building had served as mechanic shop, and the owner used to store his parts and clapped-out vehicles here. Tina had tidied it all up, built a pergola against the back fence, with paving where Rex used to practice with his harness, because back

mutations. Factors in the environment determined whether they bred with the mutated or the regular strand. It was quite extraordinary.

They were also chemical powerhouses, exuding all kinds of defensive chemicals when threatened, not that this did them any good against armadillos, because those had a very poor sense of smell.

She had even written a paper about the creatures and got it accepted into an academic journal. It would be published soon.

She was proud of the work, because no one had paid her to do it. Incredible that no one had written anything before about these remarkable organisms that could control their future breeding. Within one generation, they could become something entirely different.

Tina had released most of the experimental cactuses back into the wild, even if some kept coming back to her house, but had kept the most unusual ones, including the ones she had bred, in her back yard.

But while they were certainly curious creatures and collectors paid a lot for them, Tina struggled to see their value for someone like Simon Fosnet. Oh yes, if she still worked for the Federacy, *they* would be able to do something with the research. So would big pharmaceutical companies on worlds like Olympus, the home of PharmaCom and Schweitzer. *They* had the money to have giant gene labs. But Gandama? Peris City? No.

And these companies knew nothing of her work. The research hadn't even been published yet.

She was sure: it was not about the cactuses. This was just a way for the owner to pry into her business.

If she let him take the cactuses, that meant that he would

have to come into her back yard, and he would be able to spy on her. If he took enough lackeys to move the collection, they might even create enough chaos to steal something. Not money, but her customer database, and the names of her suppliers.

People in this place did those sorts of things. Only a few days ago, Janusz had come in and offered to work for the shop "because he didn't think Rex should be seeing customers".

Tina had asked whatever issue he had with her customers seeing Rex, and he said that "It wasn't right."

Too right, it wasn't, but that had nothing to do with Rex. They wanted to know what illegal things she did, because her business was still making a profit, and therefore there had to be something illegal.

In all of the fifteen years that Tina had lived here, Janusz had never been friendly. He was a suspicious man, always keen to get some advantage out of someone else's misfortune. He'd dress it up as "helping out", but it sounded more like helping himself.

Maybe he'd known about the lender's visit in advance because he'd met the man in town. Maybe he wanted to be close when she received the demand for the return of the loan.

Tina wouldn't be surprised if he wanted to buy the shop himself.

And as much as Tina wasn't selling the cactuses, she also did *not* want Janusz to have the shop. Because he had never done anything deserving of a favour. And he hated cactuses.

Still it didn't make sense to her that giving the cactuses, or, through them, access to the shop, would be worth forfeiting the money she owed.

Come to think of it, that whole setup smelled like a trap. And she wasn't going to blunder in. There had to be a catch, a road they wanted her to take, even if she couldn't yet see where it would lead her.

Nowhere good.

The shop was hers and would stay hers. The stock was hers. The cactuses were hers.

So she made the appointments with financial offices in town. She tidied the shop's books, cringing at those hideous red figures: ninety-seven thousand credits worth of dust.

When she came here, life in this area had been full of optimism. The hamlet of Dickson's Creek had been intended as an outpost of Gandama, with the space in between slated to be filled in with housing.

Needless to say, that had never happened. The optimism had long gone. People were leaving this area. Bands of rogues and criminals roamed the desert and increasingly infiltrated the towns. Her business might be profitable because of those very criminals, but the value of her remaining loan was greater than the value of the property if it had to be sold today. No one was going to finance this.

She leaned her head in her hands. She'd go into town tomorrow, but it was highly likely all a futile exercise.

What was she going to do? What *could* she do in three days?

A whirring noise drifted from the workshop. What was Rex doing? She'd better have a look.

CHAPTER THREE

TINA LEANED AGAINST THE DOORPOST, her arms crossed over her chest. "That doesn't look like fixing Jando Kelway's system hub."

Rex looked around. The workbench in front of him contained several metal tracks. A little wagon zoomed across it from one end to the other and back again, making the noise she had heard.

"That's boring work," he said.

"It still needs to be done." Here she was worrying about both their futures and he was playing with model trains?

"Aren't I allowed to have some fun?"

"When the work is done and the bills are paid."

"Whoa, what's gotten into you?"

"I need that system fixed. He's one of our best customers. He's coming to pick it up this week."

Rex snorted. "Yes, slave driver."

Tina breathed in heavily. The temptation to call him an insolent brat was always there, not that it led anywhere good. In better times, she probably would have appreciated his handiwork projects. He was a bright kid. But she needed all the money she could get.

"Fix it, then you can play with your toys."

"They're not toys. I'm making a system so that you don't need to go into the shed and look for parts anymore. I'm just trying it out with the toy trains because we don't have proper tracks and carriages. We don't have a robotic arm either. I'm going to make that out of some of my old toys, too. I'm just warning you."

"That's nice, but let's save it for later." Like, when the business had survived the current challenge and she was sure that there would be a shed for parts.

"Like when you spend hours trying to find anything in that mess?"

"There is nothing wrong with my storage."

"Isn't there? When I can't even go in there because the aisles are all cluttered with mess?" He gestured to the legs of his armour, clunky metal feet that were too far apart to comfortably fit in the aisles of the storage room. Shuffling sideways was not something within the armour's capability, so she had to do all the storeroom work herself. Moving the shelves so that Rex would be able to help her was one of the long-term projects that Tina dreaded, mainly because of all the superseded equipment they'd find, and the pain of having to write it off.

"Nothing that's pressing. Fixing Jando Kelway's system, however, is pressing, because it will pay our bills this month."

"You don't ever let me do anything."

Tina sighed. She didn't have the energy for this discussion right now. "You're fifteen."

"Yes, and? Does that mean I'm not allowed to have ideas?" He stuck his chin up.

He had recently acquired the build of a young man, which, combined with his arms and hands being made of metal and operated by whirring mechanisms in his shoulders, made for an imposing combination. He had recently extended the harness to its maximum height, and was now taller than she.

"Yes, much of what we do in the shop is boring. But how do you think I pay for all our bills?"

He slammed his pincer hands on the benchtop. "Oh no not that again." He rolled his eyes. "Can you ever stop trying to make me feel guilty just because of how much money you're paying for me? If you didn't want me, then why didn't you kill me off at birth? It would have saved everyone a lot of trouble."

Tina bit her tongue. For some reason, their arguments always descended to this. He thought that everything she said was a criticism of his disabilities, and that she was trying to guilt him into doing things like chores, because she looked after him and there should be something in return, right? But they were things that every normal teenager did to help around the house and he would see that if only he got over his hang-ups.

She was through with him and his stupid, childish behaviour. She pulled the hub box across the counter, with the leads still attached. "Fine, I'll fix the system myself. Don't be surprised that you don't get dinner tonight though.'

"I can make my own fucking dinner."

"Without burning down the house? Don't make me laugh. And don't go using that language on me."

He snorted, slammed his hands on the counter once more.

Tina turned to the electrical diagram, nostrils flaring. But she was so angry she didn't notice any of the tiny connections on the circuit board. And if she was perfectly honest, Rex did this work all the time, and she would have to consult the manual.

He probably knew that, too, and would say something about it.

The thought made her even angrier. Why should she have to go through this all the time? She should just kick him out of the house and tell him to look after himself, since he obviously thought he was old enough. That would teach him about all the things she had done to make his life easier.

Then again, she knew he was trying to look tough, but inside he was just a little boy. And who would help him with his harness every day? Who would carry him from his bed, and attach his artificial limbs and who would change his soiled pads and wash him?

Rex was still standing in the doorway. If his arms were flexible and thin enough, he probably would have crossed them over his chest.

"Go," Tina said. "Go and do whatever you want. Just leave me to finish this."

"I want to do something useful."

"Then help me fix this."

"Really useful."

"And you think this is not useful? I'm sorry if you think your life is boring. You can't just come and do one or two little things that you think are interesting. Life doesn't work that way."

"But it doesn't have to be so boring. Even at Kelso Station

people have much more interesting things to do than I have."

"What do you know about Kelso Station? Just because of some people you know there? People, who I add, you have never seen? What do you know about their lives?"

"Don't you think I never talk to any of the people who send me stuff? They're my friends, you know."

"I'd be cautious about who you call friends. You don't know these people. You don't even know if what they tell you is even halfway true."

"Why are you always so mistrusting? They're just other kids interested in gadgets. You say they're just keeping me away from my real-life friends. See how all my real-life friends are beating down the door?" He spread his hands. "No one's life can be as boring as mine. I get up, I have breakfast, I clean up stuff in the shop, I fix the neighbours' anti-cactus fence, for the hundredth time. I listen to them complain, mostly about you encouraging the cactuses. I sweep the floors. I do the accounts. It's boring. Bo-ring."

"That's life. It can't always be super exciting."

"I don't like my life."

"Then it's up to you to change it."

"I am trying to change it, but you always tell me I can't do things. I'm not allowed to do anything. I have to stay here and work in the shop, fixing stupid problems for stupid people. I can't drive, I can't go out, I can't dance with girls, I can't even go to school. I'm sick of it. I hate my fucking life!"

"Language."

"I don't care. I will fucking say whatever I fucking please and if you don't like it you can fuck off."

"Rex!"

"Don't 'Rex' me. You think you understand. You understand nothing. Here." With both his metal pincer hands, he grabbed the model rails from the bench. He flung the metal strips across the workshop. The little wagon that was still on the rails flew off and crashed on the tiles.

"Happy now? I can't do any more playing around. While I'm at it, let me fix this."

He walked—with a zoom-zoom-zoom of the armour—to the storeroom, leaned against one side of the doorframe and pushed with his legs against the other. The division between the office and the storeroom was not a major construction, and the wall easily gave way under his strength. The doorframe cracked loose at the bottom, and the thin boards that formed the wall broke with a snap.

"What are you doing?" Tina yelled.

"I am solving the problem that has taken you fifteen years to solve, namely that I can't get into the storeroom. All you needed to do was just make the opening a bit bigger. See?"

"Don't be ridiculous. Stop that immediately."

He picked up a length of wood.

He towered right over Tina's head, all metal armour threat and turning joints. His shoulders were twice as wide as hers, because there needed to be room inside the armour shell to attach his arms and for the mechanism that moved his arms. His hands were much bigger too, because small hands would look ridiculous on such broad arms.

The lights on his chest plate blinked to show that those arms were very much operational. He could crush planks of wood with those huge hands. She had seen him do it.

Tina rushed across the workshop. "Stop, Rex. Stop it now."

But he hefted the wood above his head, and brought it

down on the shelves. Boxes of equipment parts cascaded down when the shelf broke.

"You're breaking all my stock."

"I bet you would like to threaten me that I won't get paid. Well, I am not getting paid anyway."

"What is wrong with you? Stop it now."

Rex set his back against one of the shelves, and his legs against the other shelves and pushed both sets apart. Tina wanted to stop him, but what good was her human strength against that of Rex's mechanical arms? One lot of shelves tipped over onto the next one, making more boxes fall on the floor.

The others fell on his head in a cascade of screws and other things.

He paused, panting, and looked down. He let out a harsh breath, seemingly deflated.

"Now see what you've done. I have no time to clean up all this mess. I have no money to replace the stock. You know that man who was here earlier? He wants me to pay him back his loan. I may have to sell the shop. I have all this to worry about, and you're upset that I won't let you play before you finish the shop work?"

Rex said nothing. He looked down at the knees of his armour.

He let out a sob, and then started crying loudly. His shoulders shook while his wails echoed through the workshop.

Tina reached out her hand and pulled him up. She closed her arms around his harness as he cried on her shoulder.

But in her mind, she could still see the frightening rage in his eyes.

CHAPTER FOUR

TINA WENT into the kitchen and started making dinner. She was angry with herself for doing this, since she had said she wouldn't cook his meals, but when she worried or was angry she couldn't do anything useful so she might as well cook.

Rex had followed her, meekly and silently. He still let out the occasional sniff.

Tina felt sorry for him, but she wasn't going to tell him that.

Frankly, he had behaved like an idiot. This outburst had been the latest in a string of many that worried her. They reminded her of his father, not in a good way, and thinking about Dexter and the whole sordid mess at Charon Station never put her in a good mood.

Rex looked a lot like Dexter, too.

He sat in his special chair at the table where Tina couldn't see his face without turning around.

The kitchen drawers had handles that Rex could grip with his pinchers, and the drawers contained knives with special adapted handles so they wouldn't slip from the metal pincher's grip. The stove had a special touchpad that reacted to physical touch, rather than the warmth of human skin. With the previous version, Rex had to hold his pincher on the hot plate before the pad would turn off the element.

Yeah, that ended well.

The cupboard next to the stove held a set of metal cups and plates—Rex had too many accidents with the breakable variety—and dish towels that consisted of a wadded-up towel with a string attached, like a bath sponge, so that Rex's pinchers could easily hold them—not that he ever did.

For a long time, an uneasy silence lingered in the kitchen.

The only sounds were the ones Tina made while cutting up roots and cooking cactus fruit until it turned soft, and then putting it through the blender.

"Is it true what you said, that you may have to sell the shop?" Rex said after a long while.

"I don't want to, but there may not be another option."

"So what did that man want? I didn't quite understand that." He sounded apologetic.

"When I started the shop, I needed money to buy the land and the buildings. It wasn't much, but I didn't have any money, so I went to a creditor. He now wants to be repaid."

"Can he just do that?"

"He can. He has to give notice and I have to find someone else."

"Isn't that what loan brokers are for?"

"They are, but it won't be so simple. At the time I bought the shop, people thought Gandama would be the next Peris City and that a lot of people would come here. Houses were worth a lot more than they are now. I'm going to have difficulty finding someone who will take over a loan that's more than the shop is worth." And that was if she could find someone at all.

"If you can't find someone, then what?" His eyes were big with fear. Like this, he was so much still a little boy.

Tina shrugged. "I don't know. I'm going to talk to some people in town tomorrow. You'll have to look after the shop."

He nodded and for once didn't protest.

Rex didn't say much during dinner and afterwards said he would do some more work. It had been a long time since Rex had done that, but Tina held back her smart remarks about it. He was shaken and it showed.

She went back into the shop, too, and retrieved her computer from the drawer and went through the books. But a chunk of money big enough to repay the loan—or even just the difference between what the shop was worth and what lenders would offer—remained elusive.

She interrupted her search to take Rex to bed.

In the specially adapted bathroom, she took his harness off, took the limbs off the attachment points that were installed in the endings of the arms and legs he never had, and then his pad and the containers that collected his waste. The urine had leaked a bit and the skin had again become red. She'd have to replace the container, but replacement parts for the harness were not easy to get. She'd better put in an order now, and maybe the part would show up in a few months' time.

She washed him and oiled his skin and then she gave him a clean pad. Leaving the harness and the limbs in the bathroom, she carried him to his bed. Like this, he was still very much her baby. Then to think that having babies was Dexter's idea and she had never really wanted them.

Evelle had probably borne the brunt of that. She had been a difficult child from the beginning. Never wanted to sleep, never wanted to eat what was on offer, or at all, never wanted to listen. Had tantrums like Rex when she was eleven. Had the boobs and batting eyelashes to match.

She did well at school, but the moment Tina walked in that door from work, Evelle started poking figurative needles under her skin.

They'd sent her to the Federacy Force's officer's school to cool her down. She had gone straight into the Flight Division after that.

By now she was probably on her way to becoming a hard-nosed captain in the Federacy Force. So father, so daughter.

"Would you really find a job somewhere?" Rex interrupted her thoughts.

Tina was already sorry that she had told him about this. It was not fair to burden him with more worry. Things were hard enough for him in life already. This was her task to sort out.

"I will see what I can do. I'm sure there is a solution." Hopefully, if she kept repeating this to herself, she would find a solution. "Whatever I do, you will always come first."

He nuzzled her while she carried him from the bathroom through the hallway.

Rex still slept in the same crib she had used for him as a toddler. She had tried a big bed, but he tended to roll around and had been very distressed when he fell out one day and she hadn't heard him until morning.

She lowered him in the crib and pulled the sheet and a thin blanket over him. He often got cold outside the harness because his skin was so soft and pale.

Tina had kept his room free of invading technology. Already, there was so much metal and electronics in the house to help him. The bedroom should stay simple and calming.

One day, there would be a robot to help him out of bed and put him in his harness, but for now, she would have to do it for him.

She turned off the light in his room and walked down the hallway with a feeling of doom coming over her. Now she would need to figure out how to keep the roof over their heads.

She sat at the messy desk, her head in her hands.

All her carefully laid plans to make sure Rex could survive without her were falling to pieces. She had built the shop so that he would have an independent income. When there was a downturn, she had made up for the shortfall in security equipment sales by selling cactuses. Her plan was to pay off the loan within ten years, and then, before any potential creditors knew she had a secret reserve, access that money and buy the rest of the equipment Rex needed.

She did not want to access that reserve—besides, it would be impossible to get any money out within three days.

What else could she do? Use her reserve anyway and get a better-paying job?

A corner of a yellow envelope stuck out from under a couple of boxes. A few weeks ago, she had received that strange letter from Jake Monterra asking her to work for him. Jake had worked under her in the Perseus Agency's research facility at Project Charon, fifteen years ago.

Back then he had been shy young man, just out of training. Command told her that they employed him because he was a hard worker, but she never saw any evidence of that.

Oh, he did the work and was a not a bad young man, but reality didn't match up with his excellent credentials on paper. Of course it wouldn't be the first time that had happened.

As colleagues, they were not close. Tina didn't even think she had spoken to him specifically about her concerns with the project, and she had spoken to a lot of people. He just seemed too young and innocent to burden him with her concerns.

And here he was, writing to her to consider working for a new agency.

Tina couldn't imagine what prompted him to contact her now. It should have been clear to all that she had no interest whatsoever in returning to the employment of the Federacy Force, and that the Force probably wouldn't want her anyway.

The message had come from Kelso Station, with no further identifying details, meaning that it had probably been sent from some secret location by way of Kelso, where it had been made to look as if the message originated there.

There was no Federacy Force base on Kelso. It was a commercial station.

At the time she had dismissed his communication as just another scheme for him to get a cut of whatever employment incentives they had going on. Likely the Force needed new recruits, and he had thought an easy way out was to re-employ the ones who had already worked for the Force. Easy for him to earn a bit of money.

But was that really all there was to it?

From her memory, employment schemes and recruitment drives went on constantly. But at the Perseus Agency, the secret arm of the Federacy Force, they never had much to do with such things, nor did they have much opportunity to contact people outside the Force. The official line was that no one was to know where the Perseus Agency's headquarters were.

He would have had to make an effort to send her that. And for what? She bet the Agency's employees were excluded from the recruitment drive's benefits anyway.

Or maybe she was wrong about that.

Whatever the reason, in light of what was happening now, she might need to rethink her position. Ask what he wanted. If it was a return to space, then no way, but some jobs could be done remotely.

And meanwhile, her books weren't doing themselves. If she needed to attract another borrower tomorrow, she had to make her finances look attractive.

Gah, she'd make some tea before starting.

On the way to the kitchen, she came past the open back door.

On nights like these, when the desert chill bit into exposed areas, the cactuses would huddle up against the back wall of the house. Tina had to put pavers at the bottom of the steps to keep them from forming an impenetrable barrier into the garden. They didn't like the pavers. But for some reason, tonight, they had all remained under the pergola near the back fence.

That was odd.

Tina ducked into the kitchen to turn the kettle on and went out the back door.

The night was clear. The breeze had almost died and the sky was ink-black with a clear band of twinkling stars. Cayelle had three moons, and two of those were visible over the roof of the house. But they were both small and neither produced much light. The larger moon had not yet risen.

A faint glow to the north marked the location of Peris City.

It was too dark to see the jagged rock peaks on the horizon that were normally visible over the back fence.

Janusz's house stood to the left, but she also couldn't see it from here.

Tina inspected the area around the back door. Armoured armadillos would sometimes break into the back yard. Big and heavy, they couldn't climb, but they could dig and were strong, so they sometimes pushed over fence posts that normally kept them out. They could destroy a crop overnight, and they loved cactuses.

But no armadillo, nor any sign of one, materialised.

Yet the cactuses were distraught. Something bothered them out there.

Maybe it was the light. She turned off the outside light and turned on the light in the pergola.

Something really big—a shadow too dark to make out— ran from the area that was her mini-research station and vaulted the fence.

Holy crap, what was that? It looked like some kind of monkey. Except she didn't know any local creature that looked like that. None of the desert creatures reached above her knee.

Heart thudding, Tina grabbed hold of a broom and walked down the path. She wasn't selling the cactuses, and would certainly not let anything eat them either.

The cactuses had already started moving towards the back of the house.

Underneath the pergola, she found a container with a

syrupy substance. Some of it was on the ground, and trails of the stuff over the ground showed that the cactuses had been attracted by it. Tina scooped some of it up with a rock and sniffed it. It smelled like syrup.

What was it doing here?

It could contain poison.

Janusz didn't like the cactuses, because he said they attracted armadillos. But she didn't think Janusz would poison them. He'd had almost fifteen years to do so and never had. Had the monkey-creature left the container behind?

She took the container to the back steps of the house. Then she rolled out the hose and cleaned any trace of the syrup off the tiles.

Best to be sure.

It was disturbing, especially since Simon Fosnet had offered her so much money for the cactus collection. Maybe someone was trying to scare her into accepting his deal.

She didn't understand why he wanted them, because if he needed money for his medical treatment—whatever was wrong with his skin—then he needed to sell them first.

She should find out which collector he planned to sell them to, since they were very clearly hers, and reputable dealers would recognise her stock.

Tina was about to go back into the house when another sound echoed through the desert night—the squeak of the roller door that led into the side of the storeroom.

Someone was in the shop.

Shit. The activity out here was just a decoy.

Tina dropped the hose and the broom, looking around for a better weapon.

The only thing that remotely qualified was a shovel. She

had a gun—long unused, and when had she last serviced the thing?—but she kept it at the back of a locked cupboard in her bedroom.

That was her only thought now: the gun.

Very quietly, she crept through the garden, back to the steps to the door.

The kitchen was dark, but she knew the way. Lucky she kept chairs out of the way because of Rex.

She made her way into the hall, where it was pitch dark. Her bedroom was the first door on the right. She tiptoed into the room, all the while listening for sounds in the workshop. But it was quite a distance away.

She pulled out her trusted old Fireseed301 from the back of the cupboard.

It was the only thing she had kept from her service in the Force. Her personal weapon, now much superseded, but the chamber was full, even if it would take a few minutes for it to charge up enough to fire.

Tina took the battery out of the charging pack—she could still do this with her eyes closed and without making a sound—and slipped it into the into the bottom of the handgrip.

A tiny green light flashed on the control panel.

No matter the pride she used to take in her weapons training and her better-than-average hit rate, she was a biologist, not an experienced fighter, and she'd only ever fired it in anger at some stubbornly invasive armadillos—and hit them, too.

But even her rudimentary military training was more than most people had received, and right now, it was all that stood between the attackers and the safety of her house.

She was not going to let them harass her, and if they

thought a middle-aged woman with a disabled son was going to be easy prey, she was going to give them every reason to reconsider that opinion.

She made her way down the hallway to the workshop, putting her feet down carefully so that the floorboards didn't creak. The door to Rex's room was open, and when she passed, she heard the rustling of sheets. If he was awake, she hoped he'd remain quiet.

She arrived at the door of the workshop and peered into the darkness, listening for any sound.

Then Rex said, "Mum, what's that? What is going on?"

Someone took in a sharp breath inside the warehouse. Next there was a crash, probably of the display stand near the door into the shop. Yes, it was the display stand, because Tina could make out the piece of white foam board that displayed a selection of tiny microphones on the floor.

And the silhouette of a person, backlit by the faint light that came in from the door to the shop. Someone scrambled to his feet, bent over to gather whatever he had dropped.

She lifted the gun.

The *ready* light blinked on.

But Tina couldn't see anything in the pitch darkness of the shop. The Fireseed was only effective against living beings, because its beam vaporised water inside soft tissue. She wasn't going to waste a shot when she couldn't see.

Scuffling and stumbling noises came out of the dark as the intruder moved. The roller door at the back of the workshop was open. She guessed that was where the intruder headed.

She lifted the Fireseed so that the tiny screen of the electronic sight displayed the rectangle of the opening.

She waited.

And waited.

Was the intruder smart enough to realise what she was doing?

No. Something moved in the opening.

Tina held her breath. Come on, come on.

The intruder jumped out the back door and ran into the yard.

Tina fired the gun. The white laser beam crossed the dark space and hit him square in the back.

He yelped but kept running, disappearing into the yard.

She ran to the entrance. Damn. He was wearing armour. Judging by the sounds, he was scaling the back fence.

Tina debated whether she would give chase when she heard a familiar sound that haunted her from the past.

The charging of a plasma gun was a sound you never wanted to hear in a conflict, and one you were unlikely to forget.

CHAPTER FIVE

IN TWO STEPS and half a second, Tina had backed away from the door and had jumped inside the workshop.

Just in time. A white-hot beam of plasma hit the outside wall next to the door. Its blinding light lit up the yard and the inside of the workshop—where she could see that the intruder had pulled drawers out of the cabinet that held boxes with smaller items: clips, connectors, chips and that sort of thing.

Tina pulled down the shutter behind her, knowing that the next beam might well hit the door and would simply vaporise it. In fact she didn't understand why they hadn't already done that. Maybe it was just a warning, although there was never anything "just" about plasma guns. Especially not this one. It sounded suspiciously like a Q-blaster. Where had these criminal bandits even obtained a weapon like that? And what business did they have firing it at her? What were these people looking for? Not cactuses, clearly.

She pressed herself against the wall next to the door, heart thudding.

There were least two people, the intruder and the one with the Q-blaster. She had to be smart. As research officer, she had never received extensive military training, a subject of continuous hilarity amongst the "real" military. But she had taken pride in performing above average for the small amount of training she had received.

One thing she remembered clearly: don't rush into doing anything stupid. Most of the time, brain power trumps fancy weaponry.

Another thing she also knew: you didn't argue with a Q-blaster. The training officer, a tall, hard-faced and clean-shaven man who took no bullshit, had said about them, "If you see one of these babies, get out of the way quick smart and leave the fighting to the combat units."

She remembered wondering, what if there were no specialised combat units?

Every class of recruits had that special person stupid enough to stick their neck out and voice those questions. In her group, it was an innocent-sounding woman who had been appointed as a medical officer and was probably a lot more knowledgeable than she sounded, at least about subjects other than combat.

The training officer had looked at her, taken in her lean frame and shortness, and said, "You run, anyway."

From his room, Rex called out again, "What's going on? Mum?"

"Shhhh. Be quiet." There was not much point in saying, "We are under attack," when he could do nothing about it and she had no time to put him in his harness.

She had to make sure that the shop was safe. On a bottom shelf in the very corner of the storage room she kept a box of goodies she had collected over the years for occasions like this. She pulled it out, found the belt with the pockets, strapped it on, and filled the pockets with various items.

She had two highly illegal Expander-Z fire grenades that she had "confiscated" from a dingy shop in Peris City by showing her—expired—Federacy Force ID combined with the threat that she'd notify the authorities.

She stuffed the flares in another pocket. They were nothing more than pretty fireworks, but they could distract.

The tear-gas bombs were not going to be any good without breathing mask and tanks, and she didn't have those yet, but the road spikes might be useful, because the intruders were sure to have come here with a vehicle, and these ones contained small explosive charges that would destroy caterpillar tracks as well.

Then she put on the heavy jacket that lay next to the box. It was heavy from the armour that was sewn into the lining, and felt too hot the moment she put her arms in. It wouldn't be much good against a Q-blaster, but it would protect her from laser fire.

Last but not least, she found her IR goggles.

Kitted out, with her weapon fully charged again, she went to the front of the shop, all without turning on the lights. She made sure that the shop's front door was locked and bolted and that no one was inside—there wasn't. Then she went back to the kitchen.

The trick was to get out without the intruders noticing.

She opened the door a crack.

The cactuses had moved again and formed a protective ring around the back steps. She half expected that. The first time she had seen this, when a bad storm hit, it had surprised her, but then she figured that they might be motivated by the need to protect their source of water and shelter.

Tina crept down the steps and peered through the tangled spiky branches, but it was too dark to see much in the yard.

The night was utterly quiet, as if nothing had happened, except for the burnt smell lingering in the air from where the plasma beam had hit the wall.

The tangle of cactuses spread out from the back steps to encompass the entire back of the house, forming a protective wall. They brushed their fronds over her. Tina normally kept well away from them while they did this, because they would deposit their prickly seeds in her clothes.

But now, they gave her the cover she needed.

She slowly pushed into the mass of spikes, withdrawing her hands as far as possible within the sleeves of the jacket. This move was going to get her covered in spikes.

But the cactuses followed her.

She shuffled along the dark side of the garden surrounded by her prickly followers.

There was not a breath of sound in the garden or around it. The light in the porch was still on, reflecting from the puddle she had made when hosing the tiles.

The back fence separated the desert from the oasis of the garden. To the left, but still at some distance across a stony field, lay Janusz's house. No sound came from that direction either.

To the right stood the shed that housed the hamlet's small collection of agricultural machinery.

The person who had fired the Q-blaster must have been hiding somewhere around here. In order to fire over the fence, he would have had to stand on something, like the back of a vehicle.

She was determined to inflict as much damage as possible to the vehicle and its occupants so that they would never come back.

At the back of the yard was a gate in the fence. When she had first moved here, this was how the shop was supplied and how the previous owner had been able to store a lot of junk in the back yard.

Tina stopped at the gate. The cactuses crowded around her.

She felt in the pockets of the belt, and her hand rasped over the carpet of spiky seeds they had attached to her. They wove them into the fabric with spidersilk-like threads that were very hard to remove.

She took one fire grenade out of her pocket and hung it on the loop at the front of the belt. She took a string of road spikes out of another pocket and hung it on another loop. She checked the old Fireseed. It was fully charged and could now deliver two shots in quick succession. Then she pulled her IR goggles over her eyes.

Ready to go.

The gate hadn't been opened for a long time, and when Tina lifted the latch it creaked terribly.

Something moved in the darkness outside the yard. Tina almost fired before she realised that another mass of cactuses was crowding to get in. As soon as they realised an opening had appeared in the fence, they all started moving forward, a prickly impenetrable mass. Tina wondered how she would get all the cactuses out of the yard—and how to stop them breeding with her experimental ones.

Crouching and hidden between two flocks of cactuses, it

was hard for her to peer into the desert. The cactuses were dark—the water in their fronds made them cooler than the air. She spotted some lighter patches, but with her view blocked by the cactus fronds, they were nothing more than indistinct shapes. The cactuses might form an oasis of safety for her, but she couldn't see like this.

She straightened, allowing her to see into the desert.

A vehicle stood straight ahead, outside her throwing range. It was a type of delivery truck. A single figure stood on the back of the tray with a weapon mounted on a stand. The Q-blaster.

A second person half-walked, half-crawled towards the vehicles. What was the bet that was the person she'd hit?

Then she had a disturbing thought: did the fact that these people were still here and showed no sign of wanting to flee mean that there was a third—

Click.

A zooming sound gave away that someone was using a fast charge plasma gun, probably the Q-blaster again. Tina dropped to the ground, realising that they'd spotted her.

A flaming beam of sizzling white hot air went overhead and hit the back fence. A section of it burst into flames.

Great, she still had her reflexes. But she had fallen with one hand in a cactus branch.

Ouch, ouch ouch.

Yes, she was right. There were three intruders. And there was the monkey-like creature.

Tina wormed her legs under her so that she could rise onto her knees. She peered between the cactuses.

The figure with the Q-blaster made no effort to hide himself. No doubt he wore armour. Tina's Fireseed wasn't going to do him any harm. But there were other means of taking him and his band of thieves out.

The limping figure had reached the truck and was pulling himself into the cabin.

Tina assessed the situation. She didn't know where the third person was.

The Fireseed had two shots. She could aim one at the truck's battery, causing it to overheat, but then the two intruders would probably flee the vehicle and she had only one shot to deal with them.

She could throw the fire grenade, but she wasn't confident that she could throw it accurately enough to deliver the necessary amount of damage. Even if she did, she still needed to deal with the third person.

This called for a distraction to draw the third person back to the vehicle.

Tina found one of the flares. She opened the tube, put the flare head onto the shaft, set the shaft in the tube, pulled the launch tab and pointed the tube at the sky over the truck.

With a soft crackle, it launched.

The flare did not ignite fully until it was in the sky over the truck.

Tina lifted her goggles.

The flame bathed the desert in light. Pink light? She should have known these ones were pink, like she was having a birthday party.

Someone shouted. Something moved, really close by.

A dark shape was visible, backlit by the flames from the burning fence. *That* was the third burglar, returning to his ride.

Tina followed him in the sight of the gun, restraining

herself from firing it at him. She needed all of them in the truck.

Come on, come on, hurry up.

She moved forward, clutching the fire grenade.

The third thief reached the vehicle.

A loud crack echoed through the night. A white ball of flame engulfed the cabin of the truck. Debris flung outwards.

Tina ducked.

Holy crap what was that? It was as if someone else had a plasma gun.

The truck exploded, but two of the intruders jumped free: the man who had been on the tray and the one who had been about to get in.

What idiot spoiled her trap?

By the light of the burning truck, someone came towards her.

"What were those geezers up to?" a gravelly voice said in the darkness. Old Janusz, carrying a huge plasma gun.

The idiot. Where did he even get that weapon? "Watch it! Two of them are still—"

Tina heard the discharge before the flash erupted. She rolled back to the cactuses.

A sizzling beam hit the ground where she had just been.

"Come here," she hissed at Janusz. Idiot.

"Can't see anything," he squealed.

Shut up. With her goggles, everything was as clear as daylight.

The man with the Q-blaster had taken refuge behind a rock at the bottom of a gentle hill. The other walked in that direction. From the way he walked, he was injured.

There was nothing for it.

Tina aimed the Fireseed at the shooter's head. It would be shielded, but she needed to distract him.

She fired. As predicted, the man wore armour. The flash hit him, but his head simply ducked down the other side of the rock.

Then she pulled out the first fire grenade, pressed and held the ignition and threw it over the rock, onto the hillside.

In her goggles, she could see the grenade grow increasingly bright as it rolled down the hill until it came to the bandit's position—and exploded.

"Whoa!" Janusz called out.

Idiot.

Tina jumped out from between the cactuses, yanked the plasma gun out of his hands with a "Let me just borrow that," and ran back to the shelter of the cactuses.

The last man had turned around and came running in her direction. He might be injured, but he wore armour and he clearly had no intention of going down without a fight.

The Fireseed301 was not up to the task of stopping him, but the plasma gun was, if she could figure out this unfamiliar weapon quickly enough. It was another highly illegal piece that had somehow made it out of the Federacy's stores. Whoever had stolen it hadn't even bothered to remove the Federacy Force's Weapons ID number.

Tina was not familiar with the make or type.

With a crash and shower of glowing embers, the section of the fence that was on fire fell over.

The remaining man ran from the truck in the direction of the opening towards the house.

Oh, no, no one was going to bother Rex.

Tina fired. The gun actually discharged with a characteristic zoom that she had heard before. This was the type of plasma gun that the Federacy's planet-based forces used. The white beam hit a pack on the man's back. He shouted, and a ball of flames enveloped him.

Phew.

Tina rose from behind her shelter of cactuses.

The truck was still burning fiercely. A patch of smouldering vegetation had spread out from the place where the fire grenade had exploded.

There was nothing left of the last victim. Already, the flames were dying down.

Tina handed the plasma gun back to Janusz. "Better you get caught with it than me."

He gave her a shifty look. "I done nothing wrong."

"No, of course not."

"What? I was trying to help!"

Help, her arse. He was curious. "I had everything under control." He just wanted to see if any loot was to be had or money to be made. If he really wanted to help, there were so many other things he could have done.

He stuck the gun in his belt. "Who were they? Did you know them?"

"Nope."

"Hmm, I thought they had something to do with that fellow who was here earlier this afternoon. These characters have been snooping around all afternoon. They were hanging around in the hills, using a rented truck from Gandama, pretending to be visitors. I suspect they were measuring us up, but you don't underestimate old Janusz. They were hard to miss." He patted the gun as if he took sole credit for fighting them off.

Tina had no patience for him.

She spotted some planks that were leaning against his

back fence. She picked up one and dragged it across the dust.

"Hey, what are you doing?"

"I'm just going to borrow these until I can get my fence fixed."

"But I'm going to use those."

"You've been 'going to use those' for the past ten years. Don't worry, I won't need them for that long."

CHAPTER SIX

TINA FINALLY CAME to Rex's room, having fobbed off Janusz while staying polite but not allowing him into the house and not promising him any work. He really was annoying and persistent.

"Where were you?" wailed Rex in the darkness. "What's going on?" His voice sounded distressed.

Tina ran into his bedroom and switched on the light.

He had rolled around in his cot so that he could see the door, but his vision would have been extremely limited.

"Oh, Rex!"

She picked him up out of the cot and held him close. "It's all right. It's all right."

"Mum, I'm fine." He nuzzled her shoulder. "You're covered in cactus seeds."

True. She hadn't taken off her jacket.

"I just wanted to know what happened. I heard you going outside and I heard people shooting and then there was a fire."

"It's all fine," Tina said, patting his back, covered in a

nightshirt that looked like a bag, with the bottom and sleeves sewn shut so that the fabric wouldn't ride up his limbless body. Tina had made a couple of buttons at the front.

She felt guilty about not having put him into the harness earlier. Lying here helpless would have made her scared, too. But she'd really had no time.

He continued, "Who was shooting? What's on fire?"

"There was a burglar in the shop, but it's all right now," Tina said.

"Did they steal anything?"

"Morning will tell, but it doesn't look like they took anything important."

"Who were they?"

"Probably some band of disorganised pirates," Tina said. Although what they were after remained a mystery to her. The suggestion that Simon Fosnet might have sent them disturbed her.

"Do you know you now sound just as vague as Janusz?" Rex said.

Tina opened her mouth to protest that this was not like Janusz at all, but could see, from his point of view, that it might sound like that. She let out a heavy breath. "Honestly, that really is all I know right now. I didn't see who they were."

"Did you get them?"

"Yes." That was another thing she needed to sort out tomorrow.

"That was good, then?"

"I guess so." But the shock of it all was just starting to sink in.

"Are you all right, mum? Did you get hurt?"

"No. I'm fine."

"You went up there by yourself. Wasn't that dangerous? What would I have done if they had abducted or killed you?"

Tina cringed. It was the thing she worried about when she thought about getting old or going alone to Gandama in the truck. What if there were pirates or she had an accident and got killed? She couldn't live with the thought of Rex trapped in his cot for days, dying of thirst because she hadn't come home.

That robot she intended to buy that would help him into his harness would have to be a priority. It was the one weak point about the sanctuary she had provided for Rex, the thing that was most needed to help him to independence.

"If I could get that new type of harness, I could have gotten out of bed to help you."

Ah. There was always some kind of motive to his reasoning. Recently, the authorities had increased the hamlet's communication bandwidth for non-essentials, and now they could get several news and commercial channels out of Kelso Station. Rex had spent a lot of time looking at fully automated harnesses that were advertised to ex-military personnel who had been injured in the Force.

"Those harnesses are not for sale at Cayelle, and even if they were, we need to solve our financial problems first before I can spend that kind of money. Don't get me wrong, I want you to have one of those."

Rex gave her a baleful look. They both knew it was about more than his mobility. She knew that at some point she would have to get him a modern harness, but they were worth more than the shop's turnover for a whole year. She didn't even know if any people sold them locally. She had no money to spend on that sort of thing. Not unless they ceased to need money for food. Or to pay back loans.

Rex continued, "Next time, I don't want you going out there by yourself. I want you to help me first so that I can help you."

"You're a fifteen-year-old boy. You don't know how to handle weapons. You don't know how to fight. You have no experience. I think if you tried anything like that you would get killed."

"Without the harness, I can't run away either."

Yes, he was right, and also she had no energy for another fight about this subject.

He knew it, too, and went to dig in a bit more, as he had been doing a lot recently. "I think I should learn how to help defend you."

"I don't think you're anywhere near old enough for that sort of business."

"Then tell me who else in this house is old enough?"

"I am. And I have a lot more experience."

"We're talking about what happens when you can't be here. You just twist everything so that you can stop me doing interesting things."

"Will you stop turning everything into a fight?"

"As soon as you stop turning everything into something I am not allowed to do."

"I am protecting you. I'm doing my best. Yes, someday you will have your harness. But first we have to survive."

His face hardened. He didn't need to say anything about that being her usual response, and that never changed. She knew it, and he knew it, and things truly never did change. Because there was no money for big items like a modern harness.

And he had no comprehension of how much that hurt her.

It still didn't change the fact that the money was not there, and that the future of her business was at stake, and that she needed to find a creditor tomorrow. And to tell Simon Fosnet where he could collect his thugs.

CHAPTER SEVEN

THE ROAD to Gandama was mostly straight and riddled with potholes from the supply trucks that came to the general store every couple of days. It ran through the piece of country cheerily named Dead Tree Plain, even if the trees that had prompted the name were now so dead that they had ceased to exist. It was flat, dusty and exposed to the baking sun and the occasional whirlwinds that locals called dust devils.

Tina made her way in the old truck, having retrieved the vehicle from the shed where, begrudgingly, the inhabitants of the hamlet shared their meagre resources.

Old Janusz needed the vehicle, he said, and she answered that she'd be back before mid-afternoon.

She could have taken one of the camels, which were less in demand, but they were slow, grumpy and wouldn't allow Tina to carry supplies. On this occasion, she wasn't going to get supplies, but she wasn't going to give that away by not getting the truck. She always got the truck, so she got the truck. She'd deal with the gossip about her lack of bringing back goods later.

If she came back without supplies on the truck, they would gossip about what she had been doing. They would have known about the visitor and the intruders, because Janusz would have told everyone, and someone would work out who this visitor was. If she started asking around for someone to take over the loan, they could add up the facts.

That was the part she hated about living here.

The small community was probably still chewing on the happenings from last night, even if she had fixed the fence with Janusz's borrowed planks as soon as it got light this morning.

Old Janusz was such a gossip.

On that dusty drive—with the window open because the truck's internal climate control system had long since broken —many thoughts whirled through her mind. Uncomfortable thoughts, mostly.

Thoughts about money—or the lack thereof, and thoughts about burglars and that Rex was minding the shop by himself. She had given him instructions to barricade himself into his bedroom at the first sign of trouble. At least he was wearing his harness.

She would have taken him to town if not for Jando Kelway coming to pick up his hub, and Tina needing Jando's money. He was well off and easily annoyed. He would pay immediately, but his work had better be ready.

Jando's payment would be but a drop in the ocean of money she needed, but somehow keeping up a façade of business as usual was important to her. It kept her mind from the really disturbing thoughts, involving a position she had held, long ago, in the Federacy Force, and all the loose ends she had left dangling by disappearing, her Federacy-funded pension being one.

Somehow, some way, she needed to retrieve that money and have it paid into a civilian account. If that was not possible before a certain age, she needed to have it set up so that it would be transferred to another account at whatever the eligible age was.

But, no, she wasn't going to be able to locate and get her hands on that money before the three days were up.

There was the issue of the ship, though, and that might be a bit more promising. She had come to Kelso Station in her own ship, docked it, paid the going rate for an average visit of average duration, and had never gone back to retrieve the ship. She'd kept up with the occasional docking fee notices.

But the old boat was still there, and after fifteen years of disuse, might just be worth enough to pay for the repayment of the loan, if she could succeed at refinancing it. And she very much preferred to refinance the loan, because she planned to use the money from the ship to buy the final equipment that Rex needed once the shop was paid off. The ship was her own nest egg, and besides, it wouldn't be easy or quick to sell.

Selling it would mean going to Kelso.

That would mean having to ask Simon Fosnet for an extension of the loan terms. It would mean letting him know she owned a ship, and running the risk that he would try to extract even more money out of her.

No; she'd already decided that she'd best deal only with the loan broker and not with him. He was angling for her to contact him. Most likely, he was waiting for her angry call about last night.

She wasn't going to give him that satisfaction.

Going to Kelso would mean getting back on the radar of the Federacy and—worse—the Perseus Agency. It would mean that if they wanted to charge her—and she was sure that if they wanted to do that, they'd make up a charge she couldn't fight—they would know where she was.

It would mean facing the trouble, retracting the report on Project Charon she'd made that had prompted her sudden departure because she had refused to retract it as ordered.

But damn it, that whole project was dangerous as hell, the civilian settlers should know about it, and she wasn't going to retract it just because some military man with shiny stars on his shoulders told her so, not even if it meant having to leave her coveted and well-paid position, not even if the man was her ex-husband.

She wasn't going to retract the report, even after fifteen years.

To open a rift to another dimension was dangerous and nothing in the world would change her mind about it. Not even if the past fifteen years had proven that *this* particular rift had been safe.

And damn it, she was still angry about it.

She forced her hands to unclench from the steering wheel.

The first houses of Gandama came into view. They were blocky things, set in the dust. She needed her wits about her in case those hawkers were again following her and trying to lure her into their road trap so that they could waste her time with their sales pitches for whatever they were selling today.

But she didn't strike any trouble—they must have

trapped some other poor sod—and she reached the town's centre unhindered.

For a town of forty thousand—give or take a few thousand illegal seasonal workers—the central square was what you'd generally describe as "not much", a sorry collection of square, blocky single-storey buildings with awnings that covered the footpath so that the shoppers could walk in the shade.

For vehicles, electronic, animal-drawn or otherwise, there was the centre of the square, a hellishly hot piece of dirt where vehicles and animals were parked in no particular arrangement.

Tina preferred to leave the truck at the very edge, in case some idiot parked her in, but the bus from Peris City had just arrived and those spots were all taken by the people meeting the arrivals from the big city. So she parked on the other side, away from those casual visitors with expert degrees in cluelessness, and went into the offices of the town lenders before any of the visitors had decided that they needed to go in there, too.

Sadly, that was where her smugness ended.

To suspect that no one would lend to her was one thing, to have it confirmed, time and time again, in her face, was quite another.

What did these people know about running a shop, and anyway, why were they all half her age? If only she could speak with the agency's supervisor, she could talk them around. Some of these upstarts didn't even know what the Perseus Agency was, and why the hell did they want to know about her employment from fifteen years ago anyway?

And so, as the morning progressed—and Tina was

denied by one after the other—the prospect of having to do something radical became ever more real.

She even walked past the rental office to see what would be available for her and Rex, but none of the cheery ads said anything about wide spaces where Rex could move around freely, or bathrooms that were big enough to hold a table to wash him and a seat next to the bath so that she could hold him up.

And then she walked past the ticket office for the shuttles to Kelso Station, and kept right on walking when she saw the prices and that *prospective ticket buyers will need to provide full identification, including previous employment history and criminal records, and declare any dual citizenships.* Yeah, like that was happening any time soon. As soon as she entered her ID, the Federacy would be on to her like a leech. If Jake Monterra had contacted her, it was likely that the full bureaucracy would, too.

But she still needed the money. She had given up planning to raise the entire amount. If she could only bridge the gap between what she'd borrowed fifteen years ago and what the shop was worth today. She even considered using the truck as guarantee, conveniently forgetting that it wasn't hers, and that it wasn't worth that much.

No, going to Kelso Station and selling her ship was the only option—except it was expensive, she didn't know what to do with Rex while she was gone, and a visit to Kelso was sure to bring unwanted attention to her when she re-entered space.

On the one hand, she was only going to sell the craft.

But there was no "only" as far as the Federacy was involved. Their spies were relentless. Their mercenaries were worse.

There was no reason for them to shadow her. She was only visiting, with no intention to return.

But Jake had said the Force was looking for new blood. Positions paid well.

But she couldn't leave the shop that she had worked so hard for. And she couldn't move to town with Rex.

She didn't trust Simon Fosnet's offer for the cactuses. Besides, if it happened that she could save the shop, she still needed the cactuses to fix the hole in her budget. Then if she gave him the cactuses—which she didn't want to do—and she kept the shop, she'd forego her income from the dealer who came every month. She needed his money. If she quickly collected new stock, he would be able to tell. Already, last night's events had damaged some of her lab equipment.

Sell the ship.

But how long would she be away? Rex needed medical attention.

Damn, damn, damn, what was she going to do?

Then she remembered the existence of a place that might be useful.

CHAPTER EIGHT

ON THE OUTSKIRTS of the town lay a sprawling complex with low, single-storey buildings. In better years, it would have been located at the banks of the creek, but it was a long time since the creek had held any water, and the present dry cycle would last another thirty years at least.

These days the building lay next to a sandy patch that, with its many pipes, basins with vivid green water, and tanks, looked like a mining site.

Mining was indeed what happened here. For water.

For all that this was a desert, the ground water in the area was not deep, but it contained an unhealthy concentration of salts, which was the reason for the presence of the evaporation plant that occupied the bank of the creek.

The sprawling complex with low buildings predated the desalination plant by a few years. When people in Gandama had a relative with health problems, and looking after them at home became too much, this was where they went. A building in peaceful surroundings, with no stairs and wide corridors.

A care home, part hospital, part respite centre.

If Tina went to Kelso Station to sell the ship, then maybe she could leave Rex here for a short time. As far as she knew, mostly old people went here, but she wouldn't be away long.

Tina left the truck in the dusty parking lot at the front of the building. A few other vehicles stood there, most of them battered and dusty, except for one that she recognised as Dr Fenwicke's. He visited her house sometimes, and already looked after Rex.

Tina entered the building. The door creaked, an old-fashioned sound that made Tina think of the days she spent in her grandparents' house among the grain fields of Tirkala. A thin layer of dust had blown into the foyer, but the rest of the hall looked clean, and the woman who came to the reception at the tinkle of the bell smiled at her.

Tina asked if the facility could take care of one more person for a short period.

She was glad when the woman said, "We may have some vacancies. Is the resident mentally well?"

Tina said yes, and explained that she only needed someone to look after Rex for a short while and that it was only because he used a harness and needed medical care associated with it.

"Certainly, we can do that. I'll show you around so you can see that he will be quite comfortable." She led Tina down a corridor to the right of the entrance. "We have several levels of care, for residents who can perform their own basic functions and for the ones who can't."

"Basic functions?"

"Yes, dress themselves, clean themselves, visit the amenities, feed themselves."

She said that Rex could do only one of those things.

"Then he's a high-level care patient and his stay will be more expensive."

"I understand. It's not for long." Hopefully not too expensive. Her trip was about raising money.

"How old is he?"

"Fifteen."

"Pardon me? Fifty? That's a bit young, isn't it?"

"No, fifteen. He was... born without arms and legs." Tina hated saying that. Forever she wondered if, had she known she was pregnant, she could have prevented Rex's misfortune.

"Oh. I see. Well...we can still look after him, although most of our residents are much older. We do have a few younger residents."

"Only for a short time," Tina said for the third time.

A *really* short time, if it was up to her.

"I understand. We can definitely look after him. Come in here, this is the communal room."

A good number of the home's residents sat in the spacious room, most of them on assisting chairs of the type that could be moved into standing position so that the resident could stand up.

Tina couldn't see a single person who did not have grey hair. Most of them were wrinkled, thin with watery eyes.

Many of them sat in VR bays. They walked past a woman who was smiling and rocking to an inaudible beat while wearing a headset. A group of residents, two of them in a wheelchair, were talking into their headsets. It sounded like they were talking to each other as well as to people not in the room.

"The VR bay is very popular with the residents," the nurse said. "Wherever they come from, whatever language they spoke there, we can request scenarios that suit their tastes."

Tina felt tempted to ask if they had racing or flying games, but she was sure they would have those, too.

A few other residents sat at a couch facing a screen, watching the news at an extremely loud volume. The voice of an announcer blared through the room.

... And the citizens of Pandana have been advised to await further instructions as it is unclear what the nature of this disturbance is.

That snatch of news caught her attention.

She stopped walking. Pandana was the nearest civilian settlement to the highly secretive Project Charon. Ships that travelled to the Perseus Agency base regularly put in at Pandana for supplies. In fact, she had bought her ship there. It was the supply base that the Federacy agencies used as backup, and the commercial station owners had only been able to build under that understanding.

Disturbance was a Federacy code word for trouble. That the news report used it could be a coincidence but, likely, they had copied it off some memorandum issued by the agency. Which meant that the agency had made a public statement, and they didn't do that very often.

She waited for more information, but the announcer had already moved to another subject.

Tina felt cold.

"What's going on at Pandana that's important enough to be reported here?" she asked when she had caught up with the nurse.

"Oh, I heard something about a pirate fleet that they're

concerned about." The woman laughed. "It's a long way from here. Who cares?"

Well, she might not care terribly much, but Tina thought it was strange. Since when did the most powerful, the most sophisticated and technologically advanced military base in all of human settlement need to worry about pirates, *and* make a public statement about them?

Pirates had never been more than a nuisance, and one that didn't bother even the bigger commercial vessels, let alone the military. Pirates, or Freerangers, were poorly organised rogues, usually men, who didn't have the skill or determination to organise in groups of more than a handful, who felt lost and disenfranchised and unhappy with their lot in life.

Had something changed?

A pirate *fleet*?

She followed the nurse to the individual rooms. Each room contained a normal bed—that Rex couldn't get into—a chair that would be too narrow for him, and a wall console with buttons that his mechanical fingers would probably find too fiddly to use. At least the doors didn't have those horrible round knob handles that he found so hard to turn.

The nurse told her about meal services and laundry services—all for a fee of course.

Then she said, "Let me introduce you to Dr Fenwicke."

"I already know him."

Indeed, it was that Dr Fenwicke. He lifted his eyebrows when Tina came in.

"This is an unusual place to see you. What are you doing here?"

Tina explained her situation with Rex. "I had hoped that you might be able to look after him here, but all the residents are much older. The nurse said something about a few residents his age."

"Yes. As a matter of fact, we do have a few patients his age."

"I didn't see them."

"They usually hang out in one of the rooms. They like to talk about their own things and play their own music. I'm sure you understand."

Yes, she did. "Could I meet them?"

Rex had tried going to a normal school in Gandama, but there were no other children like him.

"Sure, I'll take you."

Tina followed him down yet another hallway, feeling somewhat happier now. Maybe this wasn't so bad a place. Rex might even make some friends.

"In here." Dr Fenwicke gestured to a door to the left.

Tina turned to the room—and stopped in the doorway.

The boy on the bed—if it was a boy—was covered in grotesque grey growths on every part of skin she could see.

Root-like branches protruded from his forehead and hung over his eyes.

He must have noticed her, because he turned his face to the door. A growth-covered, alien face.

And the protuberances were *moving*.

She felt sick. She backed into the corridor and faced Dr Fenwicke.

"What's wrong with him?"

"Her. This is Lily Basso."

"Lily Basso?"

Tina knew the little girl, or at least she had known her years ago. She lived with her parents on the outskirts of town. But the figure on the bed was *not* Lily Basso. This was some sort of mutant.

"How long has she been like this?"

"These people started coming in two years ago, and before you ask, no, we don't know what causes the skin to mutate. It's a progressively degenerative disease. We don't yet know if it kills."

And, Tina realised with horror, she had seen two more of these people: Simon Fosnet and one of the bandits last night.

"It's not contagious, is it?" She stared at the figure in the room.

"It hasn't been. But affected people are usually brought here by their families. Because their skin has a mind of its own, the victims find it hard to pick up or touch things and this makes it hard to live normally."

The girl lay on a special kind of mattress.

"They're otherwise completely normal mentally. Lily has been quite depressed recently. She would like to talk to a person her age."

Yes, Tina could guess as much, but just looking at the girl made her skin itchy. She didn't want Rex here.

"I'll have to ask my son. What if...Rex would prefer to stay home?"

"That could be possible. He may be able to get by with two daily visits of a nurse to your house and a friend you trust."

"But what would happen if he fell or got stuck?" Or if Janusz scared the nurse, or there was a sandstorm and the nurse couldn't come?

Or when thieves turned up again?

"You would need a trusted neighbour to check on him."

"I'm afraid there is no one I trust enough to do the job properly." Hell, she wasn't going to let Janusz into her house. He'd be able to rummage through everything and there would be no way for Rex to stop him.

"Then you will have to bring him here. We can definitely look after him very well."

Tina half-agreed to bring Rex and left for the truck with a leaden feeling in her heart.

Somehow she had imagined a ward filled with young people, all born without arms and legs. People in harnesses that allowed them to lumber around through wide corridors without obstacles to trip over or bump into, and where nursing staff would be on hand to help them. Where there were no embarrassing stairs that they couldn't negotiate. Where they could play silly games without feeling embarrassed, and where he would actually enjoy himself.

When Tina came back home, having dodged questions from Janusz about her trip when she returned the truck, the raid the previous day, and the fact that she hadn't brought back any stock, she found that the nurse was with Rex.

She watched from the door as she cleaned the attachment points better than Tina could and gave him his anti-rejection injections.

Lately, Rex didn't like it if Tina watched.

She remained at the door.

First the nurse took off his breastplate and his arms so that only the metal rods and leads poking out of his shoulders were left.

Then she got him to crouch over the bed, and took off the leg plates.

When the knees came off, the harness flopped down on

the bed, landing Rex on his backside. She then took off the thigh sections, so only the stumps of his legs were left.

When Rex was born, he had a little misshapen foot on one of those stumps. It had only two toes. But even that little foot had to be taken off in order to attach the harness.

Every time Tina saw Rex like this on the bed without his harness, she thought of looking at him the first time after he was born, seeing that red lump of skin without limbs, realising that he would be dependent on her forever and that her life would never be the same. And that she would be alone to face it.

The nurse inspected the joints between the metal rods and the flesh in his legs to check for infections. She applied a cleaning solution to those areas. She washed him, giving special attention to the areas normally covered by the nappy.

Through this embarrassing procedure, Rex lay on the bed staring at the ceiling.

When it was done, the nurse put his thigh parts back onto the leg rods, then the pad between his legs and the cover plate, then lifted him up onto his knees and attached the rest of his harness. She gave him an injection in a fold of skin on his belly, and then attached the arms and the breastplate.

When the nurse was about to leave, Tina took her aside.

She asked in a low voice, "How easy would it be to find someone private who could look after him full-time for a while?"

The nurse frowned.

Tina explained that she had to go away for a job but that it wouldn't take long.

The nurse explained what she could do, and, like Dr Fenwicke suggested, someone could visit twice a day. But that didn't take care of the problem of a possible attack from bandits.

She would have to hire some security guards as well and, presuming they could be trusted—which was always up in the air in Gandama—it would cost yet more money she didn't have.

CHAPTER NINE

WHEN THE NURSE LEFT, Tina made for her office.

Out of the back of the cupboard, she pulled an old box containing devices that were more than ten years old. Did this stuff even work anymore?

"Hey, mum, I asked you a question," Rex said at the door. And then, when Tina didn't reply, he said, "What's that?" He nodded at the device in her hands, an old tablet that surprisingly still worked, although it complained of low charge.

Displayed on the screen was her certificate of ownership of the craft. She copied it before the device went dead.

Rex came to stand behind her, his harness zooming and clicking as he did so. "What is that? Do you own a ship?"

"I do. If it's still there."

"You're kidding. A real space ship? Where is it?"

"At Kelso Station."

"Really? Are you a pilot?"

"I was. My licence has probably expired by now."

"In space?" His eyes widened.

"I don't know where else."

"Why didn't you ever say anything about that?"

"It's not really important." Well, at one point it had been an important part of her life, but she hadn't wanted to talk about it for years.

"Then why are you going there? I heard you talking to the nurse."

"We need money. I'm going to sell the ship."

"You're kidding. All that time you've kept it and now you want to sell it?"

"Yeah."

Put like that, it did sound ridiculous, and pushed her nose into the fact that she just hadn't wanted to deal with aspects of her old life. She'd pushed it into the "later" basket for a month, until it became two months and three, and four, and before she knew it, a year had passed, and then two years and three... And then she'd made dealing with the ship her retirement plan, and its value was going to pay for everything she couldn't afford with her shop income, but only when the shop had been paid off—just because she *didn't* want to deal with it.

He gave her a sideways look. "How do I know that you're not going back to your old job and leaving me here?"

"Because I'm not. I have no interest in going back."

"Then why did you keep the ship?"

"Because..." Tina spread her hands.

"In case you wanted to go back. I saw that you've been getting messages from someone in space."

Jake's letter. For crying out loud. Why was he spying on her? "That's my old colleague Jake. He's being the same nuisance he was when I worked with him. I don't want anything to do with it. You shouldn't be snooping in my correspondence anyway."

"I just saw it. He wants you to come and work for him."

"Will you just stop it? I'm selling the ship and I'm coming back as soon as I've sold it and have the money to pay off the owner."

"You're only coming back because of me."

"Yes! Because of you."

"Because you need to baby me."

"Because you're my fucking son, that's why, and before I murder you, let me tell you that I actually love you!" She strode through the shop and out the back door, slamming it behind her.

In the yard, the sun had set, shrouding the yard in a blue-purple haze. The cactuses had taken up their usual positions along the fence line. They'd stay there until dark, when they would start to move around. They gave no sign of unrest today.

The horizon was going hazy and the had wind picked up. There would probably be a vortex dust storm tonight. Again. She hated dust storms for the mess they made of the yard and the shop. She not only had to clean the house but meticulously take apart all the joints in Rex's armour, because the sand damaged the mechanisms that allowed him to walk.

Rex, Rex, Rex, her whole life was taken up by Rex.

At one time she'd wished he had never been born, had she been clued in enough to realise she was pregnant. But at the same time, he was her blood. This was a phase he was going through, right? Things did usually get better when teenagers grew up, did they?

The door opened behind her.

She felt highly tempted to turn around and tell him to leave her the fuck alone, but that was not how they survived.

He came down the steps and sat next to her in that

strange way he could sit without a chair. "So when are you going?"

"I don't know. I need to organise stuff. I need to ask for Federacy permits."

"I thought you hated the Federacy."

"I do." And in those two words, she encapsulated just how much she hated it. "I just need permits to visit Kelso Station."

"Why can't you sell it from here?"

"Because…" She blew out a breath through her nose. She had considered the option, but she knew for sure that someone would try to fleece her. And besides, it was hard to sell something you hadn't seen for fifteen years. She would need to clean the ship out first. There might even be some classified Agency material still in the systems.

"Dad is still with the Federacy, isn't he?"

"As far as I know, yes." Tina hadn't spoken to Dexter for many years. He'd never come, he'd never seen his son, and she had stopped sending pictures, although he had paid for Rex's first walking harness, long since outgrown.

"Would you want to go back to Dad?"

"No."

"He might have changed."

Tina said, as forceful as she could make it, "This isn't about Dad. I'm just. Going. To. Sell. The. Ship. That's it."

"Then why are you dithering so much?"

"I'm not dithering. I'm trying to organise stuff. I have my responsibilities."

"You mean me."

"Don't start that again."

"But it's true. You're looking for a place to park me."

"Yes! Because I care about you, all right?" Tina took in a deep breath through flaring nostrils. Did he ever stop?

"You're not even seeing the most obvious solution."

"And that is?"

"You could take me."

CHAPTER TEN

TINA STARED at Rex for a long time. Finally, she asked, "What do you mean?"

"You could take me with you when you go to Kelso Station. I'm fifteen. I promise to behave."

"I know you would." Well, she could hope. "But it's not as simple as that. I don't think they'll have facilities for you on board the shuttle or in the station." And there was the cost of a ticket, but at this rate, it was fast being overtaken by the potential cost of employing people here to look after him.

"I'm not that special."

"Your harness is wider than most doors in space, and your movement module can't move sideways."

"I'll go in a chair."

That was the first time he'd ever agreed to do that. "It wouldn't be easy."

"I know."

"You may have to handle some pretty embarrassing situations."

"I don't care."

"Yes, you will care. I'll have to undress you in public and do all the things the nurse just did, and people will watch you."

"OK, I'll care a little bit, then."

"When we're out there and you're tired, you'll care a lot. Believe me, I've been through this." She knew how tetchy and irritated people could get in space. And those didn't even wear a cumbersome harness.

"I can handle it."

"Even handle me giving you your injections?"

His eyes widened.

"That's the price you'll have to pay."

He swallowed. "Oh. OK then."

Ha, that shook him. But she already sensed a change in him. Maybe it was a good thing to take him. Let him prove that he was as grown up as he said he was.

She'd deal with it. Maybe she could find a cheap helper on Kelso Station. It was big enough and the stations were always full of qualified people looking for work.

During the periods of weightlessness, he would be easier to lift out of the harness and maybe he could even do it himself.

The injections... Once upon a time, she had been squeamish about needles, but that time was long gone. She watched the nurse give Rex his needles every time. She could see no reason why she couldn't learn to do that.

She just needed a steady supply of anti-rejection medicines. For how long? Would they allow her to have that big of a supply? That could be a problem, but she doubted he was the only person needing medication, so there would be a solution.

She met his eyes. "Do you promise to behave?"

"I do."

"Do you promise not to have silly tantrums and do as I say when I tell you?"

"You sound like a dictator."

"Sometimes, life in space can be like that. People get into a lot of trouble when they're stubborn."

"It can't be as bad as all that. I watched all the vids, mum. It's a civilian station, not a military base."

True. And she understood that even the military bases were becoming more friendly and people-oriented, less grey and monotonous. "I don't have time to chase after you."

"I know that. I promise to behave, really." He placed his huge metal pincer over his breastplate. "Metal hand on my metal heart."

"OK, then."

His eyes widened. "Really?"

"Really."

"I'm going to space?"

"Yes."

"I'm going to space, I'm going to space, I'm going to space!" He bounced up the steps and around the kitchen, landing with a heavy thud each time. The plates in the cupboard rattled.

"Be careful. I want there to be a house for us to come back to."

"I don't care. I'm going to space, I'm going to space!" He bounced through the hallway, into the workshop, out the roller door and into the yard. "I'm going to space, I'm going to space!" And into the pergola where the cactuses waited to be watered. "Do you hear that, oh my planet-dwelling spiky friends? I'm going to space!"

Tina couldn't help but smile. Once she had been that

wide-eyed kid. Maybe it would be good for him. His life here *was* very isolated.

"Mum, mum, do you have anyone's stuff that needs fixing before we go? I got my 3D printer online and I can *print* new connectors now, a hundred of them if you want, and I'll do it all before we leave."

"I just want you to help me tidy up some things," Tina said. The subject of his printer had come up a few times. It was not that she didn't like him playing with it, but she highly questioned the legalities of the models he used, and there was a reason all her stock came from Peris City: because the printer there held the licences for all these commercial models. People got prosecuted for illegally downloading them.

"I'll tidy up anything you want. Including my trains."

"Let's have dinner first, and think about how we're going to secure the shop while we're gone."

Rex wanted to help her cook.

That hadn't happened for a long time. During the preparation and eating of dinner, she outlined all the ways they could secure their business. She said her main concern was the stock and the cactuses.

"What about the house?" Rex asked.

"If someone wants, they could burn the house to the ground, and there is nothing to stop them doing that. We still own the land. We can rebuild, because we have insurance, but if someone steals the stock or the breeding stock of cactuses, we have to start all over again. I want to store both somewhere else. At least the most valuable items."

She had done this before, of course, leaving a valuable asset in storage for a rainy day. It was just this asset they were going to sell.

Tina said that one of her suppliers hired out storage compartments. The cactuses she would have to hide in a secret valley in the desert. She'd keep the seeds separate, of course. Then she had another thought: her armoured jacket she'd worn last night. It was full of seeds. She'd take the jacket on this trip. So that was triple backup for her breeding stock.

The next morning she contacted Simon Fosnet. He was not impressed that she couldn't have the money in time for him.

"I thought I was pretty clear. I said three days."

The vid from Peris City was blurry, but Tina had the impression his condition was getting worse.

"Yes, but I need a little bit more time."

"My offer for your collection still stands."

"Thank you, but I've checked with other people. The cactuses are not worth that much, because they don't all belong to me."

"Oh?"

"The rarest ones are on loan from someone else, and because there have been some break-ins, I have returned them to their owner, since I'd hate for them to get stolen."

His face was so badly affected with the growths that it normally didn't show emotion, but now it displayed an expression of surprise.

Ha. He'd hoped she would cave on the cactuses after the intimidation team he'd sent. But she was not going to give him the satisfaction of complaining to him about the raids.

The rest of the day, she and Rex packed the most valuable stock into boxes which she then drove to the outskirts of town to a storage unit. Rex even came to help her, and didn't complain about having to have his harness disassembled to fit into the truck.

She left a variety of items on the shelves, but to the familiar, it would be obvious that this stock was easily replaced, second-hand, superseded and worth little.

She debated boarding up the windows, but decided that the usual bars across the door and windows would have to do, because boarded up buildings screamed *burn me down* to looters and other miscreants.

It even occurred to her that when she finally owned this piece of land, she might replace the ramshackle construction with a nice new building if there was any money left over. The lack of construction work around Gandama meant that builders could be hired cheaply.

That night, she sent a message to the administration of Kelso Station.

I am the legal owner of a ship docked at your facility. I am about to visit the station in order to sell the ship.

She gave them all the details.

She immediately received a long document with terms and conditions that were more familiar to her than she liked to admit. The memories of her old life were everywhere. With Rex travelling with her, she might even have to tell him about some of them.

CHAPTER ELEVEN

TINA WRAPPED up all her outstanding orders and sent messages to her regulars that she would be away. Then she secured enough medicine for Rex. This was harder than it should have been, because the hospital was not in favour of her taking Rex on this trip—after having smelled the possibility that she might pay for his care—and she had to find another clinic that would sell her what she needed. She got the nurse to teach her to do the injections.

She had some reading to do. Things had changed a lot in the world of space travel and for the people who lived in the space stations. You needed permits for everything, and needed to book accommodation ahead of time. She got the permits, needed to renew her citizenship and apply for a number for Rex, and booked her accommodation. The prices were ridiculous.

But once she'd sold the ship, she would have plenty of money.

Then Tina was left with one painful task. She collected the truck from the shared equipment shed. She drove it up to the back fence of the yard. When she opened the back gate, the cactuses in her yard had all moved close to the house.

Tina had to wrestle her way through the prickly mass to get to the hose. She turned on the tap and made a trail of water across the ground from the house into the truck. The bottom of the truck bed did not hold that much water before it started running out, but it was enough to lure the cactuses up the ramp and into the truck.

Then Tina drove her precious load out into the desert.

If she was going to leave them, she might as well leave them in a safe place, away from the town where armadillos hung around. She'd leave them in her secret place where she knew they would survive and where she would be able to find them when she came back.

Out on the rocky trail, driving slowly because no one came out here, Tina remembered the roughness of the place that had attracted her to this planet in the first place. The rock formations were just majestic, even in the hot midday light. There were still a lot of wild cactuses, huddled in groups between rocks, because this was where moisture congregated when it condensed on the cool stone at night.

As she came past, a number of them started following her.

She was sure that this had something to do with the load in her truck, but her research had so far failed to unveil how these things communicated with each other. In her early years with the Federacy Force, she had studied many of the biological life forms on settled worlds, but these crosses between plant and animal truly had no parallel anywhere in the universe.

About an hour's drive out of Dickson's Creek, there was a

valley full of strange rock formations. It looked like a giant hand had reached down from the sky and deposited random piles of giant marbles. The rocks were all of a pale yellow colour. It made it look like the entire valley was a field of budding mushrooms.

The sky was deep blue, and the rocks that bounded the valley were pink. The sand in between the rocks was white. Here and there grew some strange looking plants, like palms with thick bulbous trunks. Tina had checked them on previous occasions, and found them to be proper plants, not ones that moved like the cactuses, which seemed to be restricted only to the area around Gandama.

The most important thing about the valley was that if you looked in between the rock stacks, you'd find little bits of water.

The stacks were often taller than a house, and because each rock was round and quite big, there were huge gaps between them, big enough for a person to enter.

It was inside these piles that she had found most of the cactuses, in the dazzling sunlight that fell between the boulders, that created patterns of golden light and shade that could confuse and disorient a person.

A lot of stories circulated about this valley. If Janusz were to be believed, a father and son had once gone missing here, about thirty years ago, and they had never been found. "The place is haunted," Janusz said.

Other people had told her their communication wouldn't work in the valley—which wasn't true, although reception could be a bit dubious—and they had seen strange lights and heard strange noises. All those reports were unproven, of course.

But Tina liked the valley. She used to come here with

Rex as a baby when he refused to go to sleep, and she would just put him in the truck and drive him around the desert and show him the magical places, even though he was far too young to understand their beauty.

Today, she was here to ensure the safety of the cactuses. People who could find this place would either be locals or have an interest in the desert.

She stopped the truck in the middle of the rough track that went through the valley. Once the rush of air and the hum of the engine had stopped, a blanket of silence fell over the area. The air was hot and pressing.

Tina let down the back gate of the truck. "Out you go." She said it more for herself than because she thought they would understand.

The cactuses moved down the ramp onto the dusty ground. One or two started towards the nearest pile of boulders.

The wild cactuses that had followed her remained at the top of the ridge. They appeared more rugged to her, with some of them damaged from armadillo attacks. Others had dead branches.

Her cactuses all remained together in a group. They did this when they were unimpressed with the situation. Tina almost felt guilty leaving them to their own devices, even if they had originally come out of the wild before she started breeding them. Some of these half-plant-half-animal creatures were hundreds of years old. She made a short recording of how they all stood in the desert.

With sadness in her heart, she climbed back into the truck and drove home. She hoped she'd be able to find all the cactuses again when she came back. If they were smart, they'd disperse and hide. People were dangerous. The cactuses were much better off out here than in some warehouse under the care of someone in Gandama who knew nothing about them.

Then there was the last of the packing up to do. Tina cleaned the shop floor and windows, so it would take a while before the place started to look dusty and abandoned. She took all her information off the computers: the latest financials, the customer database with everyone's addresses, security system types and passwords. She put this information on a datastick to take with her.

She did the same with all her research data from the cactuses, including information about the breeding, and where she had found the cactuses.

Then she locked the shop's storeroom at the front and the back.

Standing in the shop, Tina remembered all the things she had experienced here. Putting Rex in his harness for the first time, and watching him learn to walk. She remembered his laughter and squeals when he realised he could jump and use his pincer hand like a bat to hit balls.

This was where Rex had unpacked his birthday presents, and where he had done his schoolwork.

She remembered him raging about the kids at school for the short time that he went there and, mostly quietly, working away at reading through some information about electronics.

"Are you ready with the shop yet?" he asked from the door.

"Almost. Can you take all our stuff to the truck?"

He went into the hallway and picked up both of their packs at the same time. Rex's medicines alone weighed quite a bit.

He gave her a sideways glance that said, *See, I can be very useful.*

Yes, the harness made him stronger than a normal human being, even if he was less agile.

Tina followed him outside, realising with every step that she might have secured her business but, when she came back, the building might not be here.

CHAPTER TWELVE

IT WAS TIME TO GO.

Rex didn't fit in the cabin and he didn't want to be disassembled to fit, but he was happy to sit in the back tray with the bags. He was smiling.

But Tina's heart ached when the vehicle pulled away from the shop—all dark and shuttered up. She was prepared never to see the building again, but she hoped nothing would happen while they were gone.

Janusz watched from behind his gate, stone-faced. Tina hadn't told him where she was going other than a vague story about a medical visit to Peris City. The fewer people knew, the better. Especially Janusz. He would start snooping around when he knew for certain that she wasn't going to be back for days.

The hamlet of Dickson's Creek receded in the rear-view mirror. Soon all she could see was a cloud of dust that followed the vehicle down the road.

The bus to Peris City left from the town centre in front of

the bank. When they arrived, it was already waiting, although none of the passengers had climbed on board.

It was busy in the central parking lot, with people doing their shopping after work. The sun was still hot, its glare blinding.

Tina parked as close to the bus as possible. Janusz had told her to drop the keys at the bakery, so someone from Dickson's Creek could later pick the vehicle up.

They joined the queue for the bus, whose doors were still closed.

The passengers belonged to a varied group: older people who would be travelling to see friends, visit children or go to medical appointments, and men or women travelling alone who might go for business or job opportunities. A group of adolescents Tina couldn't place were a few years older than Rex, and they seemed to be travelling together but without being part of an organised group.

Rex hardly came into town, and he attracted a bit of interest. It was only a small taste of what was to come.

The driver came out of a sandwich bar and opened the door so that passengers could get on, but immediately there was a problem: Rex's harness didn't fit through the front door.

The driver had to take out a side panel so that he could be lifted inside, by Tina, with help from the driver and another man, since walking steep and narrow stairs was also not one of his capabilities.

Rex didn't say anything through the ordeal, but there was thunder on his face whenever he caught the attention of the group of adolescents, who hid their curiosity poorly.

Rex had to stand at the back of the bus, too, because there wasn't enough room in between the seats for him to occupy a normal seat. Tina wanted to sit on the control box next to him, but the driver would not have it. All passengers needed to be safely restrained—Tina with a seatbelt, and Rex with luggage straps.

This was not a good start, but true to his word, he said nothing.

Tina ended up in a seat next to one of the adolescents, a young man from Red Peak, another small farming community close to Gandama. He told her that he and a group of friends from school were going to sign up for the Federacy army.

"Do people still do that?" Tina asked. It was how she had joined herself, since her family had also lived in a farming community.

"They were advertising for people to join. The pay is good, and they teach you a trade. I was just bored at home, annoying my parents. Not much else to do on the farm. The robots do all the work and Dad looks after the robots."

"Were they recruiting for a particular reason?" Tina asked, thinking of the news segment she had seen in the care home. When she joined, the Federacy had been expanding their services.

"The recruiter didn't say anything special, just that there would be training and if you signed up you'd travel to a lot of places. Seems like a good way to do it. I don't have any money to travel otherwise."

He seemed disturbingly innocent. Tina had been a bit older when she signed up. Surely she hadn't been so gullible?

The bus took the best part of a day to get to Feris City. Since it was now mid-afternoon, most of the trip was at night. Because of its three moons, the night on Cayelle wasn't particularly dark. The moonlight, a sickly kind of grey, turned the landscape colourless. Peris City lay in the mountains, in a landscape even drier than Gandama, where the main industry was mining.

Tina stared out the window, watching the mining installations whizz by with their processing plants, big mountains of rocks and loading stations. Most of the mines were day and night operations and brightly lit work sites stood out in the night.

She thought of the first time she'd travelled to Gandama on the bus, broken, with a disabled child she had mixed feelings about, and looking for a place to hide from the world. She had found it in the backwater of her security item shop in Gandama, where there was no direct connection to the Federacy and where she thought no one would bother to come looking for her.

The place had grown on her, but there were times that she hated the person she had become, cutting herself off from everyone, including Dexter and Evelle. Evelle would be a fully fledged captain by now, out in deep space, flying the ships and helping the Force's logistics. And she would say about her old mother, *She lives in Gandama out of Peris City on Cayelle. It's sad.*

Tina had seen recent photos of Evelle, but when she thought of her daughter, she could only remember her red-faced, screaming obscenities at Tina in the hallway of their unit at the staff quarters at Project Charon.

Tina knew mothers weren't supposed to feel this way, but it had been such a relief when Evelle got into the Federacy Force boarding school at that horrible age of fifteen, when she'd done her utmost best to make sure her family hated her.

She had almost succeeded.

Still, Tina had tried to contact her to say that her parents had split up, and later that she had a little brother. But Evelle had never replied.

Rex was now the same age. Tina glanced at him sideways. He had fallen sleep, and the pale moonlight lit one half of his face. He had been so good and mature the last few days. She was proud of him. One day, he would be able to live independently, and it was all because he was a smart kid with a good heart, even if he could sometimes be a little shit.

Not like Evelle. He was nothing like her.

They came to the outskirts of the city when it was starting to go light.

Peris City was the pearl of the Kappa-665 system, plainly known as Kappa, a solar system that included Cayelle and four uninhabitable planets. Built about fifty years ago, the city was pretty much in its original design, with the circle-and-spoke approach to planning. The residential areas were still on the outside, and the spaceport was at the end of one of the spokes.

By the time the bus stopped there, most of its other passengers had disembarked. Space travel was expensive and people who lived in Gandama had no reason to do it, because they wouldn't know anyone to visit and had no business at the stations.

But the group of adolescents also got off here, which meant that they'd gotten a space placement. That was definitely odd. From Tina's memory, they didn't usually send new recruits into space straight away. It must mean that they really needed people.

The uncomfortable thought of hearing about an attack on Pandana returned. She hadn't been following the news.

When you lived on a planet, stuff that happened in space quickly became irrelevant. She had enough trouble keeping up with politics on Cayelle.

Tina remembered Peris City as a worn grey dust bowl, but the modern airport precinct they entered was nothing like her memory. Clean streets with neat paving, glass and concrete buildings, bright signs, shopping malls with stores selling brands she had never heard of, huge warehouses with electronic gadgets.

Things had changed a lot.

To be honest, it frightened her. What if Kelso Station had changed as much and she didn't recognise the place?

"Look at the plants," Rex said. It was the first thing he'd said since they had left. Hopefully this meant that his bad mood had gone, because Tina felt in no state to deal with that.

The plants were indeed magnificent, big healthy specimens, with healthy lobes in brilliant green, not the red-tinged scrawny things in the back yard in Gandama. Tina had thought those ones looked healthy, but they had nothing on these.

And for the first time since leaving, it looked like Rex was enjoying himself.

Tina had booked accommodation in a place near the spaceport. This was another place she hadn't been for a long time and looked nothing like she remembered.

They had been given a room on the twelfth floor, but since Tina pointed out issues with getting into the lift and negotiating a set of steps in order to get to the room, she managed to get a room on the ground floor. The room had a little garden, and Rex wanted to go outside. His harness could only fit through the narrow screen door sideways—the width of this thing was becoming very annoying— and she managed to twist him around and push him through. It was hot work and she realised that she would have to do the same to get him back inside again.

That was too much to face before dinner, so she decided that she was going to pick up a quick dinner in one of the surrounding eating-houses.

As she walked through the hall of the accommodation, a news flash came over the screen in the hall.

The attack on Pandana has left the other stations in the area vulnerable to the enemy. The military forces at Charon have been left unprepared and understaffed. For now, everyone in the area has been advised to leave.

A few people stood watching this, but most ignored it.

A chill crept over her. A big conflict was clearly going on, but no one spoke of who or what they were fighting out there in deep space.

And she was taking Rex with her to travel back to that world?

Another thought: Dexter and Evelle were still alive, weren't they?

In her mind, she saw fragments of a broken station floating through space. She might have lost contact with both of them, and she might call Dexter an arsehole whenever she got the chance, but wishing him dead was an entirely different matter.

Evelle, too.

One day, she intended to make it up to her.

Tina bought some food at a stall and took it back inside. Everything about this place was new and alien to her. Fifteen years was really a long time.

When she got back to the room, Rex had discovered the

outside camera views that allowed him to look out onto the city. He had an eyepiece that could enlarge sections of his vision, mostly to look at very small things, but he was wearing it now and studying the projections in great detail.

For the moment, he was commenting on all the things he saw, his voice excited. He briefly looked over his shoulder when she deposited the containers on the table but for once did not seem particularly interested in food. He continued to talk about all the things he saw.

He pointed at a dot in the sky. "Look over there, that's an X model, do you see it?"

"Dinner is here."

"You're not even listening to what I'm saying."

"I have to think about a lot of things," Tina said. "Like keeping you fed and cleaned. Come over here so I can change you."

That got his attention, and he reluctantly submitted to the procedure of being dismantled and having his private parts cleaned. The day in the warm bus had not done the skin on his backside any good.

She worried about the upcoming trip. How would Rex really react to the claustrophobic corridors and cabins of the space stations and ships? He was used to being outside. He wouldn't have his freedom. Quite a large area of the station and the ship would be totally off limits. How was she going to keep him occupied?

CHAPTER THIRTEEN

THE SHUTTLE WASN'T due to leave until mid-morning, but Tina was glad that she got up early, in the pale light of the morning while it was still cool.

Getting to the shuttle was a hassle, and that was an understatement. The bus that took them from the terminal did not have enough room for Rex's armour, so the only way to make their flight, for which Tina had paid dearly, was to take the armour off, and take Rex separately onto the bus.

She had to carry him, and to be sure, a boy with no arms and no legs got a fair bit of attention from the other passengers. Unfortunately, the problems didn't stop when they left the bus, because the contraption didn't fit in the shuttle either.

Because the safety harnesses in the shuttle seats were designed for people with arms and legs, it didn't fit properly, so Rex had to be put into some sort of bag structure that could be put on a hook on the wall. The flight attendant showed Tina how to put it on.

She wrestled Rex into the bag in the narrow space, while

the people who had to sit on the chairs she was using waited in the aisle, which meant other people couldn't get through and some were making comments like *Please hurry up, other people want to get to their seats, too.*

When she finished, it turned out that some other occupants in bags already hung on the wall. None of them were over a few months of age.

Rex's mood did not improve with having to share the space with a number of noisy babies.

Tina got a seat one row back from the wall. It looked kind of ridiculous, the row of all the small babies with small heads and Rex with his adult sized head and face that he would have to shave sooner rather than later.

The flight attendant had at least been considerate enough to give him the spot next to the window. But the people facing him looked very uneasy.

Tina offered to swap seats with one of the couple.

"I'm his mother," she said.

The woman said, "Oh. I don't understand why they didn't put you with him."

Well, Tina didn't understand why the shuttle didn't have provisions for people like Rex, but that aside.

The woman was keen to move to Tina's seat so that Tina could be with Rex. Or be the one to listen to his unimpressed muttering.

But finally all the passengers were seated and strapped in, and they were ready to go, and his mood lightened a little.

Just think of it, he had never even been to Peris City, let alone to the spaceport, and his interest in technology was such that he keenly watched all the different kinds of craft parked at the dusty spaceport. He even knew the names of some of the models, so for a while the talk was all about that.

He wanted to know what models she had flown. It was the first time that he had shown any interest in her previous career.

They didn't speak a word about their dusty house and the shop, but Tina missed the cactuses already. She wondered if they had survived the lonely night in the desert or if the armadillos had ripped some of them to shreds already. Or if the collectors were looking for them.

Finally the shuttle was ready; all the luggage was stowed, including the components of Rex's harness—and Tina kept a close watch on where the crew put those—and they were ready for takeoff.

The trip only took two and a half hours, but the station orbited in such way that departure was only possible during certain windows, and the shuttle did not deviate from those.

It was a long time since Tina had felt the pressure of rumbling engines and the pressure on her chest from being taken out into space. Of course a passenger shuttle was very different from a private craft, especially a military one, since those usually had more powerful engines. But the feeling brought back a lot of memories nonetheless.

Rex was mostly silent during take-off. Not that the engine noise allowed people to talk freely, even if some of the babies had different ideas. The infant hanging next to Rex had gone bright red in the face.

But it wasn't long before they came into familiar territory for her: to see the horizon recede, the sky turn dark and the limb of the planet appear as a hazy blue arc through the window.

Two of the planet's moons appeared above the horizon.

Rex looked at them. They would normally be seen

tumbling through the sky at nighttime, chasing each other across the firmament at crazy speed.

Had she ever seen the full round moon on Earth, he wanted to know.

Tina hadn't, but Dexter had. At some point during this trip, they were going to have to talk about Rex's father and his sister. Rex knew that he had a sister and that she had a function in the military. He didn't know any of the circumstances that had led to their breakup and Tina's departure from the Force. When he was a child, she had simply told him that she no longer wanted to stay. That answer would not satisfy him as an adult.

Why had she left space?

Why had she given up a successful career?

What was it about people that they would sometimes deeply betray those who trusted them?

She wasn't looking forward to these discussions.

In any case, he seemed to enjoy the trip so far, and mentioned the bright speck at the horizon that was Kelso Space Station long before the announcer made the comment that they were about to arrive.

Tina almost didn't recognise the shape of the station. In her time, Kelso had been a simple one-ring structure, hovering over what was a backwater world, where there was no customer base for a large trade hub in orbit.

In the time since she had last visited, the station had grown two new rings, and by the look of things, the location of the spaceport had been changed. They now used a central system, where all the ships docked at a post attached to the axle of the ring structure before moving them out of this position to a docking rig, making it possible to dock and undock more than one ship at a time. This was more common in larger stations, and Kelso was no longer a small station.

She wondered what all those people were doing here. Besides some mining, Cayelle was not a popular world, and its deserts did not contain desirable export products. Unless you counted sentient cactuses.

When arrival at the station was imminent, the ship went into a holding pattern that was also very familiar to her.

While circling the station, she looked for places where private ships would be docked. The shuttle port, to the left, she could clearly see from her window. The new port included lots of rigs and structures off the main rings where various ships and mining technologies were on display.

Two large ships were docked at the outermost rig. At that size, with that space-weathered surface, they could only be Federacy warships. She had never served on them, but she thought—from distant memory—that this was a Norway class vessel. So, these huge, serious warships came to Kelso these days?

What were they doing here?

Again, she thought of the group of young people from Gandama. Was the Federacy increasing its presence in this area?

From this distance, she couldn't make out a specific shuttle docking area for the much smaller private ships but she assumed that her ship was somewhere out there amongst all those little specks and tubes that glared brightly in the sunlight.

In all, she was impressed with the size of the place and a little intimidated. Somewhere in the back of her mind she realised that it might not be that easy to find her ship. The port master would certainly know, wouldn't he? Then again the man who had been port master in her day would probably have retired and there would probably be a port office with more than one employee to deal with this many ships.

And then it occurred to her that she had not received anything except automated replies to all her messages to the Port Authority and the fuelling station. Any ships that looked like they had been abandoned, if their owners couldn't be contacted, were usually sold to the highest bidder at regular auctions. What if they had sold the ship off, because they deemed that they could no longer contact her? Dickson's Creek was such a backwater, she wouldn't be surprised if messages didn't always reach her.

The ship might not even be here anymore.

CHAPTER FOURTEEN

The shuttle docked with a soft clunk, and an automated voice started a prerecorded message to welcome all new passengers, telling them to make sure to take all their belongings with them and all that sort of stuff. Most of the people got up from their seats and started collecting their things, some of which had managed to move quite a bit during the trip. Because they all got up and queued in the aisle, Tina couldn't get through to the back where Rex's harness was stored.

As a result, Tina and Rex were the last ones off the shuttle. The crew needed to unpack Rex's armour, Tina needed to put it on and then they needed to wheel all their luggage out of the craft.

By the time all that was done, most of the other passengers had left, and only the crew still stood around the exit tube.

In fact, the officers standing around were joking with

each other, and were surprised to see some final passengers coming out.

The appearance of Rex caused some raised eyebrows.

The customs officers took Tina's ID and asked her some questions. Where she was going, what she was doing at the station, and how long she was staying.

Once, long ago, she would have sailed through these types of checks. She would have had a pass that let her through the fast lane. One look at the badge on her chest and they would have known she was from the Perseus Agency, and those people were treated with utmost respect. Now she was just another citizen, and the process felt humiliating and unfamiliar. She didn't like it.

Somehow, she had to restore some of her former identity passes. Ex-service personnel had certain privileges, even after they left the Force. She should see what she could still access.

Rex studied the gadgets held by the officers closely. He seemed to have overcome the embarrassment of having had to travel with his armour off, and his curiosity took over, even though the officers gave him strange looks. Tina almost snapped at them, *Have you never seen a person in an exoskeleton before?*

Some of those people used to work at the docks, Tina remembered. Most of them had been involved in accidents. Didn't they have accidents anymore? Was space really so discriminating that only able-bodied people came here?

The officers studied Tina's and Rex's civilian IDs, wanting to know where *Gandama* was, and sounding incredulous that someone from there would come up here. But finally they let Tina and Rex through into a long corridor with bright ceiling lights into a hall with lifts around the perimeter.

First they needed to find their accommodation. According to Tina's memory, the accommodation quarters were close to the entrance of the spaceport. But the only exit from the hall was into a long lift that went into the weightless part of the middle of the station.

She had forgotten about that. The spaceport was not in the same place it had been before. They entered the station in a different place. She might as well be on her first visit here.

It was busy in the spaceport, and the lift was crowed. Once they left the hall, everyone inside the lift slowly became weightless. Rex had to hold himself onto the side, but his size made him awkward and he couldn't stop his harness bumping the woman next to him. She gave him dirty looks.

Once they were in the space station's main hall, Tina recognised where they were, even if much had changed there, too.

The somewhat old-fashioned and dingy hall had been replaced with a modern open commercial area with shops and restaurants and many of the station's authority offices. They came past the trade office, the military office, and the Port Authority office. She would have to visit that one later.

They arrived at their accommodation, indicated by a sign in garish pink neon lights that said *The Weary Astronaut*. Even when booking the service, Tina had found it a strange name, since hardly anybody still used the quaint word astronaut anymore.

People streamed in and out of the main door through the establishment's dark lobby, out the lifts, past the desk and into the commercial passage. Some guests went out a glass door in the back of the lobby, where Tina could see a dining area with faux plants made to look like a garden, with tables and chairs like outdoor furniture.

The lobby itself was small and every bit of wall space was covered in old-fashioned posters of humanity's first forays into space. The Mars landings, the first commercial space station and, heavens! the first Moon landing.

"Wow." Rex stopped to look around.

Tina went up to the desk and gave her name. They had received the reservation, and they gave Tina an access card.

In the lift to the top floor of the establishment, Rex said, "I thought you said that this place was expensive?"

"It *was* expensive."

She hated to think what cheap places would have been like. As it was, Rex barely fitted through the corridor, which was dark with scuffed lino floors and scratches along the walls where people had tried to move large objects.

She opened the door to the left, and stopped in the doorway.

The room was barely big enough for the two beds that stood in there. Just a tiny space was left between the wall and the beds, barely wide enough for a normal person to walk, let alone someone wearing an exoskeleton.

"I would have expected a bit more comfort for my money," Tina said. It was clear this room would never do.

Once they put their luggage down, there wasn't even enough space to walk. "I'm going back to the reception to see if they have anything better," Tina said. She shut the door again and, with Rex following, went back into the lift.

A group of people had arrived at the reception. They were all quite young, and spoke with a tone of bravado that made Tina sure that they were military personnel of some description, even if they did not wear uniforms.

She and Rex had to wait until they had all been allocated rooms. They stood in the corner of the tiny lobby area, trying to keep out of the way of people walking into and out of the place. Some of them knew the group that was checking in, and lots of noisy greeting ensued.

Two people walked past, one of them wearing an exoskeleton like Tina had never seen before. It allowed the wearer to walk normally. It was dark blue and gleaming. Little lights lit up along the legs and in the hips as the various parts engaged.

Tina couldn't even work out whether the person wearing it was disabled. It looked like an arrangement that people would wear just for fun. The man's steps were bouncy, almost soundless, none of this clonking and creaking that Rex's harness made.

Rex stared at the man until he disappeared inside the lift. Then he looked at Tina. It went without saying: that harness would be small enough to fit in between the wall and the bed. It might even be able to shuffle sideways.

He said nothing, but she could see the longing in his eyes.

He looked ancient and battered in his old-fashioned harness, and she finally realised that this was why people in the station had been staring at him. They'd been wondering why the piece wasn't in a museum, considering him some sort of apparition from the past.

The group of military personnel had gone from the reception area, and it was Tina's turn to go up to the counter.

"What can I do for you?" the woman behind the desk asked.

"Do you have a larger room?"

"That will be difficult. As you can see we are very busy."

"But my son doesn't fit in between the bed and the wall. I did tell you in my application that I needed extra room."

For moment, the woman looked at the screen to find Tina's details.

"That's right, you did. I assumed that he was wearing a normal exoskeleton."

And she looked at Rex as if he was something from another dimension. "Is that part of a costume or something? Or are you trying to sell it to collectors?"

Tina gave her the iciest stare she could manage. "The application didn't have a box to enter dimensions for the space we needed. I assume that people wear different types of harnesses depending on their conditions."

"Oh. No, I didn't realise that. I suppose we should change that."

Another curious look at Rex, because now, clearly, something was wrong with him much worse than what was wrong with all the other people who wore exoskeletons at Kelso Station.

Great.

But in the end, she allocated the pair of them a room on the ground floor, much bigger—and much more expensive —than the first room. It had two double beds, and a desk and a couch with a small table, a fridge filled with all kinds of snacks in bright colourful packaging, and a bathroom marginally bigger than the other. Washing Rex in that cubicle would still be an issue, but this was much better.

"There is nothing wrong with me," Rex said, standing in the middle of the room. "They're talking about me like I have some sort of horrible disease."

"I know. It's just that people need to feel sorry for you."

"I walk, I can run, I can jump, see?"

He jumped up and down, landing with a heavy thud each time his metallic feet hit the ground.

"Yes, yes, I know."

"No, you don't know. Everything on this trip is about me, about how silly I look with all those babies, and how embarrassing it is that I don't fit in seats. And that I'm wearing a costume and I should be in a museum."

"I did warn you."

"No, you told me about having to give me my injections. That's about me again. About the *disease* that is me. Why don't you just toss me out the airlock and be done with it?"

"Just stop it, will you? I'm tired, I have no energy for this."

"Do you think about me? Do you think I have energy for this?"

"Stop it. You can either shut up or I will send you home."

That did the job. In the end, neither of them could change anything, so Rex fell quiet and said nothing, while Tina suggested they go and have a look around the place and maybe find something to eat.

Something to eat was always good, and lately, she had noticed that Rex was crankier when he was hungry, so they left the room, went out to the hotel lobby, where it was still busy, and into the passage outside.

CHAPTER FIFTEEN

COMPARED with how Tina remembered it, the commercial area of the station was modern and quite spacious, with a tall ceiling and glass-fronted shops and a gallery level that overlooked the main passage.

The lighting was diffuse and warm, made to resemble afternoon sunlight. Here and there stood plants in pots, although they certainly weren't plants from the planet below.

Tina and Rex wandered around the main commercial passage and its narrower side alleys with their quaint shops and service offices.

So much had changed here that Tina barely recognised it. Back when she came here last, the commercial area had been old-fashioned, with claustrophobic, low ceilings and shops that operated in rooms that resembled freight storage areas.

If she hadn't known any better she would have judged that she was in one of the larger stations.

It was busy in the passage. The tourists from the planet

were easy to pick. They were the people in the space over-alls, because somewhere the rumour went around that one needed to wear one of those suits, so the tourist companies got their charges to wear them. They also walked slowly in groups, getting in the way of the locals who just wanted to do their shopping.

Tina started noticing a lot of military people. They were in the bars and the restaurants, talking and laughing in groups. Even when they were not in uniform, they were obvious to Tina. She knew the way they stood and the way they talked to each other, and she recognised snatches of the jargon drifting through the general noise of the station.

There were a lot more shops than last time, or at least during her last visit she hadn't noticed them so much. When everything you needed was supplied to you by your employer, you didn't take notice of places where you could buy things.

They were real shops, too, not the old-fashioned hole-in-the-wall where supplies of identical items lay stacked on shelves, like a utilitarian warehouse or supplies room. These were shops with display stands and clothes racks, with sales assistants and change rooms. There were electronics stores with flashing screens and even homewares stores that boasted everything for inside apartments or ships. *We adapt all furniture to measure,* one store sign proclaimed.

"Hey, look at this," Rex said.

He had stopped at a well-lit shop window, almost pressing his nose against the glass. On neat, clean shelves lay a collection of gadgets: mini consoles, comm devices, and a host of other things.

Most of them sported worn edges, scrapes, or other signs of use, but there were also some newer devices of a type Tina had never seen. Strange and new technologies already being sold second hand. A whole generation of electronics had passed her by. On the surface of Cayelle, they just didn't get many of the technological advances that the rest of human settlement enjoyed.

Rex said, "If I could get that screen, I could set it up so that you can watch who comes into the shop from the front door. Look, they even have the control unit."

In a much less neat cabinet inside the shop lay an array of outdated computer equipment, the cables all jumbled up. The shelves behind it contained a variety of home entertainment units.

"It's a pawn shop," she said.

"What's a pawn shop?"

"It is where people who don't have money go to sell their possessions so that they can have money to pay their creditors."

"You're saying it like that's a bad thing."

"No, it isn't bad per se, but it's usually associated with a less than savoury crowd."

His eyes widened. "You mean some of these things are stolen?"

"Probably, or obtained in other dubious practices."

She remembered stories about people being forced into debt and people preying on the estate of elderly people who had no family on the stations, so that when they died, all their possessions were taken and sold before the family knew about it. It happened a lot, especially to people who were not poor enough to have no possessions, but not rich enough to be able to afford a trust company.

"I want to look inside," Rex said, having forgotten the quest to find something to eat.

Tina wouldn't normally want to be seen dead inside a shop like this but, on the other hand, she had no great plans for this afternoon, and looking around the shops was better than sitting in their room at the accommodation.

So she went after Rex into the shop.

It was cramped and crowded inside, and his harness did not fit in many of the narrow aisles. To help his customers, the shop owner had arranged all the interesting items around the main aisle that led up to the counter.

While Rex looked at all the most recent models of the latest gadgets in glass-fronted cases, Tina walked through the narrower passageways. The shop owner stood at the counter at the very back, waiting to come out and bother either of them ready to be parted with some money. It looked like the shop had plenty of supplies, but was short on cashed-up buyers.

Sure enough, the man came out into the main aisle and started chatting with Rex. He asked where he was from, what he was doing here, and Rex answered all the questions honourably, that he was here with his mother and that she was here for work. Somehow the man smelled money, even if Rex had none of his own and wasn't old enough to sign for purchases anyway.

Tina wandered deeper into the shop. Soon enough, Rex would see how annoying these people could be. Let him learn his lesson in a less expensive way than she had learned it.

The back aisles of the shop contained shelves with equipment that was not in glass cases. Sometimes they were household items, and sometimes they were electronic items from an age she remembered.

At one time she had genuinely enjoyed working at the

agency, because they did groundbreaking work. That was when she met Dexter, a handsome military officer in a spiffy uniform. In the pale bleakness of space, Dexter's deep olive skin and dark hair had made a dashing appearance. His intelligence had been a refreshing change from the straight-laced military officers that she had spent most of her service years obeying.

It was a trip down memory lane. She remembered having used a comm device like that one. It had been the one Dexter had used to propose to her when, surprisingly, she had fallen pregnant with Evelle.

Rex's voice cut through her thoughts. "Mum, come and have a look at this."

Tina had better rescue him from the shop owner.

He was standing near the counter, where soft light emanated from a glass case. The shop's owner stood behind the counter again. Likely he had figured that Rex wasn't old enough and he was wasting his time.

In the case, on a spotlessly clean mirror, behind a spot-lessly clean pane of glass, lay a gun. It looked brand new.

It was a fairly powerful weapon of the Fireseed range. Not the old 301 that she had, but a newer 312 model, the type the Federacy would issue to recruits who had passed their weapons training. The barrel was smooth, without the typical Federacy Force engraving.

The markings had probably been polished off.

She wondered where the owner had gotten this weapon.

Rex said, "He says it's 10,000 credits, and that he can't talk to me about it, because he can't sell to minors."

"And he would be right. That is no thing for a boy your age." Tina tried to sound as casual as possible, as if finding a recent, very powerful gun in the pawn shop was a normal thing.

"But isn't it pretty?"

"Guns can kill. They're never pretty."

"Gah, you're boring."

"I'd rather be boring than dead, or in prison."

Whatever this weapon was doing here, it was highly illegal, and she wanted nothing to do with it. She didn't even want to give the owner the impression that she knew it was illegal, or that she was even remotely interested in it.

"Come," she said. "I'm hungry. Let's find a place to have dinner." And she bundled him out of the shop.

"But I still want to look inside," Rex protested.

"That was an illegal gun, and he knew that I knew that it was an illegal gun. You do not talk or look like you're interested in illegal guns in a place like this."

"But then why did he display it in such a nice case?"

"Because he was asking a lot of money for it, and probably because he wanted to showcase it for his usual customers. People like us, honest people, don't come into shops like this."

She looked over her shoulder, but it was too busy to see if anyone had noticed them coming out of the shop. At any rate, they would be clearly visible on any security footage, for those who kept an eye on these things.

She was already sorry that she had succumbed to Rex's curiosity. Nothing but trouble came from interacting with these people.

CHAPTER SIXTEEN

FOR DINNER, Rex insisted that he wanted to eat the space food that he had read so much about: space burgers, station loafers and dock signs.

Tina hadn't the heart to tell him that despite the ridiculous names, the food wasn't all that great. The closest any of it had been to meat was the gloved hands of the poor person putting these delicacies together from recycled protein. Rex would probably regret it the next day, but she left it. The garishly coloured displays on restaurant menus hadn't changed terribly much in the past fifteen years, even if the style had been updated.

Whether you ordered soy burgers or sausages, the food was all fake. Even copious seasoning couldn't mask the taste to Tina. It brought back unpleasant memories from the time when she was supposed to lead a secret life and wasn't allowed to interact with people outside the agency. Only rarely did she come to Pandana Station—which was much like Kelso Station—while on duty.

Most types of artificial food were not kind to Rex's delicate digestive system, and of course space heroes never got nappy rash.

They ate at a rather noisy and bright place with garishly coloured seats and smooth tables. Next door was a cute place with the theme of Cayelle: oranges and rust reds, a floor that looked to be made of dirt, and even some cactuses, standing in their pots like terrified rabbits. On closer inspection, Tina found them to be fake.

Tina pointed it out to Rex, but he just snorted.

He didn't like Cayelle. He wanted something different. It was a feeling she knew well. Once, she had left her family. She'd liked to think they were horrible and boring, but her parents had raised four children in their home and were still happily together. Her brothers were all happily married with beautiful families and successful businesses. Only their ungrateful youngest child had taken off to space and never come back. Only their youngest child had made a mess of her marriage and family life, and even knew there was any such thing as fifteen-year-olds getting nappy rash in space.

She was through with trying to put on a façade. She already missed Cayelle and the cactuses. She even missed the nighttime howling of the armadillos and the dust storms. It was familiar. This station belonged to a world that was no longer hers.

The restaurant was full of military personnel. She explained to Rex that they were Federacy troops, and then she needed to explain that the Perseus Agency was the spying arm of the Federacy Forces. He wanted to know if she wore a uniform when she worked. He seemed disappointed when she said that she did, but that the uniform didn't have a badge of a flying horse.

"We were not supposed to be easy to recognise. We were

meant to look like everyone else. It meant uniform when we were on duty, civilian clothes when not."

"Then who were you spying on?"

"Mostly internally, other departments. Different worlds. Some of them were always trying to skim off materials and influence local politics."

"So you were spying on your own people?"

"Pretty much. What else is there to spy on? Aliens?" A feeling of unease crept over her. "But, to be honest, I wasn't in that division of the agency. We worked in the science division on a thing called Project Charon, an anomaly in space that we were studying."

"Like, an alien thing?" Rex's eyes were wide.

"Not really, but a phenomenon that people didn't understand."

"Sorry, is this chair taken?" a young man asked. He wore a Federacy Force uniform, with Flight Division insignia and officer pips labelled Engineering. He was older than most other personnel hanging around and had a friendly, olive-skinned face and dark hair with flecks of grey at the temples.

"No, it's not. Sit down. We were about to finish," Tina said.

He sat. "You don't have to leave for me. Finish your food." He grinned. "I don't bite."

That was so typical of flight troops. They were most likely to encounter civilians because they travelled the most, and had the mantra that they were the face of the Force drummed into them.

"Are you expecting more people?" Tina asked. Usually these people came in groups.

"No, it's just me today. My mates were on duty." He grinned again, in a most disarming way.

But when all your mates were on duty and you couldn't find anyone to go with, that was when you ate on board in the mess, right?

He continued, "We've been in port for weeks, with no word on when we're being sent out. The official term is *patrolling the area*. But I'm an engineer, so there's not much to do. The situation on the ship is getting a bit tense, so I wanted to have a quiet meal by myself while meeting some of the locals."

He was either new to the Force—but then his ranking didn't make sense—or genuinely curious, or—something else. Tina didn't know what. Innocent? His attitude was almost naive.

He held out his hand. "Anyway, my name is Finn. Flight Engineering Officer second class, SS *Stavanger*." His nametag, which military personnel had to wear, said F. Kaspari. That rang some bells with her, but she couldn't remember where she had heard the name before.

But the ship, Tina knew. The *Stavanger* was one of the Norway series, likely the one she had seen when coming into the station. Those were serious warships with thousands of crew that were an entire ecosystem of their own. "Nice to meet you. I'm Tina Freeman and this is my son Rex."

His mouth fell open. "You're kidding. You're *the* Tina Freeman?"

Heat rose to Tina's cheeks. "I don't know. I'm sure there are plenty of people with that name."

"From Project Charon, right?"

Well, shit. "I worked there, but it's a very long time ago." She did *not* like the way this was going.

"You worked under Dexter Freeman?"

She cringed. "He was my husband, but if you know that much about me, I'm sure you know that also."

Rex was watching with wide eyes. Tina rarely spoke about his father. She just didn't see the point of transferring her bitter feelings about him onto her son, even if Dexter gave no intention of wanting any contact with Rex.

Finn shook his head. "It's such a pity."

Tina's heart jumped. "What is? What happened?"

He frowned at her. "You don't know?"

"I left rather suddenly. I have not kept in contact." That was putting it mildly.

He gave her a strange look. "The project was closed down," he said.

"Really? Why?" Tina felt she already knew why, but she wanted to hear it from his mouth: they took too many risks and something went wrong. People were killed.

"No official explanation was given, but the Force cordoned off the sector, and then spent an extraordinary amount of effort and money chasing a couple of pirate ships. The rumours have it that a band of pirates managed to steal something from the project, but none of us know for certain. This is all public rumour, by the way. You should be able to read about it on the news channels, if you want."

Well, that was not at all what she expected to hear. And it sounded, kind of... stupid, to be honest.

"So you're saying that somehow some pirates managed to break into the project and steal something valuable from the military? Something so valuable that they're spending a lot of effort chasing after it?" If true, which she doubted, it would be a severe embarrassment. The Perseus Agency and especially Project Charon was the most secure and secretive facility in the Federacy Force.

Finn snorted. "That was pretty much how it went. Of course the pirates didn't like the Federacy's sudden interest in them and started to organise themselves in groups in order to survive and fight back. They formed an ever-increasing fleet that has been growing ever since. They have grown into a formidable force that the Federacy now has to contend with. The conflict has gone much further than retrieving what was stolen."

Wait—conflict? With pirates? And it all had to do with Project Charon? Tina remembered hearing about the Federacy fighting pirates on the news channel she happened to listen to while in the care home at Gandama. She couldn't imagine pirates making any kind of impression on the Federacy Force.

"What did they steal? Does anyone know? Did they get it?"

"No one knows, but it seems unlikely there was a resolution, because there has been no change in our orders. Mind you, they don't tell us anything in the first place."

"So the pirate story could be nonsense?"

"It's what we heard from people who were on the ships who got to chase pirates, who were a lot of people. No one told us what the pirates had done beyond *trespassed in a prohibited area*."

Tina laughed. That was such standard vague Federacy language for things like this.

Finn laughed, too. "I know, right? A lot of people speculated about reasons that they kept talking about pirates. The Federacy never liked pirates so it might be a way to keep them quiet."

Few people liked pirates, but there had to have been a good reason to go after them. The Federacy had signed all the human rights agreements, and never allowed anyone to forget that.

"These pirates, who are they? Do we know names? I presume they come from established worlds. Do they operate on planets as well?"

"It seems likely. They call themselves the Brothers of Anarchy. They have leaders, no doubt, but none of us know who they are. They tend to operate in smaller cells and each of them has different aims. I dare say that some of them can be quite law abiding and interested in trade."

"So that's what you're doing here with the ship? Protecting the station from pirates?"

He grinned. "That's the official line. As usual, and as you will know, the Federacy Force does not pass up an opportunity to increase their size and influence."

Yes, Tina knew that. Even Jake Monterra's letters about employment now started to make sense. "The Federacy is officially expanding its influence into this area under the guise of chasing pirates?" Of course they would like to hire an employee who didn't require a massive amount of training, who already lived locally.

"They're trying to push into areas where they've not been active recently, to make sure that the eligible young people sign up for the Force rather than join the pirate army."

"Are the pirates recruiting?"

"If they are, they're likely to use alternate methods of doing it that few people know about. So we're doing it openly to prevent pirates getting a foothold."

Tina thought of the young people who had been on the bus to Peris City with her. "You said that Project Charon was closed. What happened to the Perseus Agency and Project Charon?"

"The agency is still going. The project was closed down, the sector was cordoned off and is a no-go zone at the moment. They're still working on what to do with Pandana, since it is constantly under attack from pirates. I don't know what happened to the infrastructure that was part of the project. I suspect that the small research station is still there, or has been towed somewhere else where the Federacy can use it."

She knew that station inside and out. She had lived there for the best part of six years. "What about the people who lived there?" She couldn't bring herself to name Dexter and Evelle, but for some reason, after fifteen years, she worried about them. About Dexter because she didn't want to run into him, and about Evelle because she'd been avoiding Tina, not answering her correspondence, and she was her daughter, after all. Evelle probably hadn't been to Charon for a long time, but it was where Tina planned to start looking, when she was ready to face the nest of hornets that was Evelle.

"Most of the personnel got relocated to different divisions. If there was a research opportunity for them to work, they went there but, in reality, most of them went into the Flight Force."

A chill went over Tina's back. "Do you have any of them on board your ship?" She didn't want to run into anyone familiar when she didn't expect it.

"Probably a few. I don't know anyone in particular."

They ate for a while in silence.

During the conversation Rex had been silently listening. He now met Tina's eyes. It was hard to figure out what he was thinking. He had never shown much interest in his father. He knew about the existence of his sister, but since that question about whether she had been born with arms and legs had been answered in the affirmative, he hadn't shown much interest in her, especially since Tina couldn't describe her in any other way than "difficult to get on with" in every aspect.

But he had to be thinking something about them. What was it with these teenage boys and their deep thoughts?

They finished their meal talking about the facilities at Kelso Station. Finn was much more familiar with them than her outdated map. He said not to bother with any of the shops in the main commercial area. If they wanted to buy something, it was much better to go to the trading room where goods and services were traded at fair prices between the customers who actually used them.

"Thanks for that information," Tina said. "In all honesty, I'm here to sell an old ship that I've had moored here for a long time, and I probably should have sold a long time ago but I just couldn't be bothered. I need some money back on the planet for my business, and if you know of someone who wants to buy a ship, I've got one for them."

"You have a ship?" Finn said. His eyes widened. "What model?"

"It's only a GenTrac Omega-6, about thirty years old. It was a decent solid thing but I haven't used it for a long time. There are likely to be a few things wrong with it."

"Those are very solid ships. They don't make them like that anymore. You're unlikely to find anything major wrong with it."

"I just need to clean it and fix it up so I can sell it."

"You'll find plenty of customers," Finn said. "A lot of people are scared of pirates and hate the thought of being stuck on one world or a tin can like the station."

"Then I might be lucky for once."

After they finished their meal, Tina and Rex went back to the hotel room, where Tina had to deal with washing Rex, a job she had neglected over the past day or so. In places, his skin was going red from being sweaty in the harness too long.

She would have to look after him better.

Rex asked to use his entertainment system for a bit, so she propped him up in bed facing the screen that he controlled with movements of his eyes while she ducked into the shower.

When she finished, he'd fallen asleep.

Tina eased him off the pillow and went to turn off the screen. He hadn't been watching a movie, as she'd assumed, but studying a wire model of the GenTrac Omega-6, with the controls and navigation units magnified.

Tina sat on the couch in the corner. She idly paged through pictures of her cactuses, wishing she were back home. She opened her pack and took out her armoured jacket, unrolled it and looked at the array of seeds stuck to the fabric. The station's quarantine office would have a fit if they knew they were here, but rolled inside the jacket, they had escaped detection. Hopefully the cactuses were coping. Hopefully no one had found them.

Hopefully no one had yet set fire to the shop.

She looked through the station's port log, or the part that was public. The SS *Stavanger* was mentioned there, and it listed a crewmember under the name Flight Engineer F. Kaspari.

She then searched for the Kaspari name, and found why the name rang a bell with her. The Kaspari family owned a huge stake in the Olympus settlement, an industrial complex on the world of Olympus. Tina had never been there, but she'd heard many rumours about the money and influence that members of the family sought to buy.

She was never terribly interested in gossip, but her search uncovered sordid stories of the family's patriarch George, who was married four times and had seven children by four different wives. The children were all in conflict with each other and their respective mothers. George had a brother called Michael, and he had been investigated for corruption, most notably under the serious charge of trying to buy influence into the Federacy assembly, headquartered on Olympus, that oversaw the Federacy's administrative processes. They were a dry group of people that no one worried much about, but who wielded enormous economic power, even if it was done mostly anonymously.

Michael Kaspari was suspected of having tried to bribe one of the assembly members.

She looked around the family tree, and found a number of people in the younger generation who were called Finn.

One of them was clearly a child, because the birthdate was given, but about another, not much detail was given. This was a son of George's second oldest child with his first wife.

She wondered if that was the Finn Kaspari she had met, or whether it was a common name.

And then she wondered why such an influential family would find any benefit in sending a son to do a fairly low job on a large but ordinary warship in an out-of-the-way section of the galaxy.

On second thoughts, probably a lot of people were called Finn Kaspari.

She looked up photos of the fabled Kaspari family

members, and did not see any obvious similarities between them and the man she had met. There was one photo of the entire family at some sort of gathering, and there were a lot of children in the picture, but they were not all named.

At any rate, why should she care? She had a ship to sell and a business to get back to.

CHAPTER SEVENTEEN

BUT FINN'S words disturbed her more than she wanted to admit. Project Charon had been closed down, and he might be content not knowing why, but she definitely wasn't.

She searched for the information and found that it was as Finn had said. The reason for the closure had not been given, but the regular Federacy Force had swept in with their big ships and had wreaked havoc on a fleet of private ships in the area, widely assumed to be a pirate band.

Pandana, the nearby civilian station where she'd bought her ship, was under quarantine.

Fancy that. So much had changed. She also found out that, back in her day, it had been okay to call pirates Freerangers, but these days, that was a loaded term, because it was what the pirates called themselves with pride. They were free of the tyranny of Federacy rule.

In the morning at breakfast, she told Rex that she was going to do some boring administrative jobs and that he was free to watch some movies until she came back.

"Where are you going?"

"I need to go to some offices to do paperwork."

"Can't I come?"

"You'd find it really boring."

"Oh, okay." He sat back on the bed, looking a bit disappointed.

She promised she'd be back soon.

Walking through the station without Rex was much quicker. Because his harness was so heavy, he was also quite slow and often needed to wait until people moved out of the way. She could take the stairs, rather than having to wait for the lift, or wait for Rex to slowly lumber up the stairs. She felt a little guilty about thinking about him this way, but it was probably best to do these boring jobs by herself.

But she hadn't gone far when she had the feeling that someone was following her.

At least two men walked behind her who stopped when she stopped, when she observed them in the reflections of shop windows. Both were quite tall, wore dark nondescript clothing. One of them wore a fake pirate belt as fashion accessory. The metal studs and eyelets glittered in the light, but nothing hung from them. One had short hair, balding on top, and the other had long black hair tied in a ponytail. He also had a goatee.

Tina was baffled why anyone would follow her. Were they people who had seen her looking at the gun in the pawnshop? Were they just random thugs? Did they, like Finn, know who she was?

She turned around and walked the other way, only to see the two men disappear into a shop before she reached them.

Then she went around a corner and walked through another passage parallel to the commercial centre.

Kelso Station wasn't big enough for commercial areas

multiple blocks deep, so this second passage was much quieter.

The men did not follow. Tina kept looking over her shoulders, but they had probably taken some sort of shortcut and would be reappearing in front of her any moment. She was looking so much over her shoulder that she didn't see the man who came out from one of the doorways. She almost crashed into him.

"Oh, sorry," she started saying, but then the man exclaimed, "Tina Freeman!"

She stared at the man.

He had sandy hair, blue eyes, and wore a uniform with a Kelso Station Authority emblem on the chest.

She didn't think she knew any people who worked here. But his face was vaguely familiar.

"You received my message?" he asked.

Tina was about to ask which message when it dawned on her. "Jake Monterra?"

My, he had gotten quite a bit older. When he worked in the lab for her, he had been a skinny young man, a student, assigned to her by the Perseus Agency as a brilliant new recruit. But he had been shy, never saying much and fearful in the face of other people who knew so much more than him.

"What a coincidence that I bump into you right outside my office. I didn't know you were here. You should have replied that you were coming, and I would have given you a tour."

"I have some matters to attend to," Tina said. She didn't quite know where to begin with him. They had never been close. Yet meeting him here might be her ticket to get out of this sticky follower situation. If she could get him to accompany her to the commercial passage, any of her followers would give up, seeing his uniform.

"You're safe?" he asked.

What an odd question, given the situation. "Yes. Why not?" Did he know she was being followed? Had he arranged it?

"You were walking very fast. There are a lot of unsavoury types around in these corridors. They hang around here because we're close to the employment office."

"I'm just a bit lost. I followed some people down a set of stairs, I thought it was a shortcut to the shops, and now I'm not quite sure how to get there. Maybe you can show me while we talk."

"Sure."

They started walking slowly.

He asked what she was doing and Tina told him that she had only recently heard that Project Charon was closed.

"The person who told me didn't know that much about it. What happened?"

"The usual. Someone in the head office decided they needed to make budget cuts."

That was not at all the way she'd heard it. "What about the invasion of pirates?"

"Oh, that was after we moved out. The Federacy troops needed to come back to sweep the area, but there was nothing major and we weren't affected."

"It was quarantined, including Pandana?"

"That's correct. Just to make sure that no one was selling contraband agency equipment."

That was a very different story from the one she had heard, and she didn't know how far to push for the truth, or if it was even her place to do so. If the project was closed, who really cared?

"It was sad the project closed down," Jake continued. "I found it quite difficult to find employment. I wasn't yet graduated, and suddenly a lot of people were on the market looking for work. I was glad Kelso Station offered me a position, even though it's obviously not in line with my studies."

"I hope you finished your degree since," Tina said.

"Not yet, but I'm working on it." He smiled.

"After fifteen years?"

"It's a busy job."

"What work do you do at the station?"

"I work in quarantine, mostly with non-food animals and plants. Not so far removed from what we did at Charon. But what about you? You disappeared rather suddenly. One day I had a supervisor and the next I didn't."

"I had a disagreement in vision over the direction of the project," Tina said.

It was rather strange talking with him like that, because surely he would know much better than she ever could what had gone on at the agency after she left and the disturbance her departure would have created.

"They appointed Grello as your replacement and life went on as before. Not much was said. They were very professional about it. Dexter said that it was a personal matter and should not affect the operation of the project. And it didn't. We all went on with our lives."

Business as usual. How typical. "Did anyone tell you why I left?"

"There were some rumours. Mostly that you took up a relationship with someone else."

"That's utter rubbish." Tina couldn't say anything for a

few seconds because of her anger. Dexter had made it about her. He had not discussed her letter to him with the staff because he had been uncomfortable with the content. Jake was clearly Dexter's pawn, either by choice or ignorance.

She took a few calming breaths. "So then they closed the project, and what did they do with it?" Tina had to find out whether anyone had taken any notice of anything she said.

"Dexter and a few people who joined after you left took over the business part of it."

"Business part?" Tina said. As far as she knew, the project was completely non-commercial.

"Yes, that's what I'm doing here when I'm not working for the Kelso Station Authority. I'm developing the business that came out of the project. That's why we could use you."

"And Dexter still works in this business?" The hell, no.

"He does. But he's not the only one."

"And what about Evelle, does she work for them, too?"

He squinted at her. "She left to join the fleet. Dexter mentioned once that she serves on the SF *Manila*. As I already told you, Dexter works in the company but I don't see him very often. Grello is still my main boss. He was keen to hire you."

"Well I'm quite busy and I'm not keen to go back into space," Tina said. She wouldn't want to work for these people if her life depended on it.

"It might not be a space-based position."

"No, thanks. I'm fine."

"Is there anything we can do to entice you?" he asked.

"Not really. I have a business on the planet below. I'm happy."

"Is that the Gandama address that I sent my message to? You have a nursery, right?"

"Like a plant nursery? Goodness no. Most of Cayelle is desert. I have a business selling security equipment." But how did the nursery idea get into his mind? Those cactuses again.

"You did read my message?"

"Yes, I did. Thank you for that, but I'm not interested in taking up a position. I'm quite happy with my business."

"But I already said you could stay right where you are, work for us from your home. We would send people to visit you occasionally."

Like Dexter? Hell, no. "I'm much too busy with my business."

"But you do have time to write research papers?"

Tina's heart jumped. "I'm not sure what you mean." How did he know about that? The paper had been accepted but not yet made public. Unless he had some academic position, which he had just admitted he didn't because he hadn't even finished his degree.

"Weren't you involved in genetics research with some of the native wildlife?"

"I run a shop. Selling security equipment."

"But you're a biologist."

"I *was* a biologist when I worked for Project Charon."

"You worked with alien wildlife."

"I know what I did." Seriously, what was this about?

"We can use a biologist. You can work in your research field again. We have started a project researching Cayelle's sentient plants."

"For what aim?"

"Research? Is any further aim necessary? We don't know what those creatures are. They're alien, and we want to understand them."

"A company doesn't do anything without the potential for a financial gain."

"Sure, but we don't know what that gain will be."

"But you've got something in mind?"

"We have all sorts of things in mind, but right now, the work is a blank canvas. Imagine the freedom of being able to determine your own research. Didn't we always dream about that in the lab? No more cost-benefit projections, no more juggling project funds, no more boring meetings justifying your work to people who have no idea what you're talking about and aren't interested. Just pure science."

Sure. Pardon the sarcasm. "And who is paying for this again?"

"Our company. When you visit the station, you'd have all your expenses covered, and wouldn't have to stay in a cheap place either."

Another chill. Did he know where she was staying? No, surely she was being paranoid.

Jake sounded very innocent, but all Tina could think about when she remembered her work at Charon Station was the cloud of particles coming out of the rift. Jake wouldn't have seen that cloud of particles, and reports about it would have been very much suppressed by those in command, like Dexter. "Really, I am not terribly interested or looking for work. My business is doing well, and I have other responsibilities."

"Oh, have you remarried?"

"I have responsibilities." Tina didn't want to go any further than that. She was looking for a way out. She'd sort of liked the young kid Jake when he had come to work in the lab. He'd grown into one hell of a persistent salesman. She didn't trust him.

They had been walking slowly while talking and now they had arrived at the beginning of the commercial passage. Tina thanked Jake for helping her find her way, and he told her to make sure that if ever she changed her mind she contacted him. She said she would.

And then Tina walked through the passage as fast as she could. She looked over her shoulder, sure that people were still keeping an eye on her, but it was too busy to see.

She was supposed to have been doing boring stuff, but this encounter had been anything except boring.

CHAPTER EIGHTEEN

WHEN TINA WAS as sure as she could be that Jake no longer watched her, she stopped to note "SF *Manila*" on her PCD.

SF stood for Star Fighter, an attack ship, much smaller than the behemoths like the *Stavanger*, which were glorified troop carriers, command centres and logistics providers. The Star Fighters did the work, and the ones of the Southeast Asia class were at the forefront. Their whereabouts were a secret. Their missions were a secret. Weapons they carried on board were secret. No wonder she'd been unable to find any information about Evelle other than some really generic stuff.

Evelle had just turned thirty. What would be her function on the *Manila*?

Whatever else had changed at Kelso Station, the office of the Port Authority was still more or less as it had been before. Nothing had changed about the large, low-ceilinged waiting room, where hundreds of people waited to be served at the counter at the far end.

Tina got a number from the old-fashioned machine, and sat down to wait.

Next to her, a couple of merchants were arguing over which of their allocations they would use for which part of their fruit. A couple of hawkers were plying their trades in the room. They were watched in turn by a number of security guards.

Tina knew that selling wares to people who were waiting here was not allowed, and the security guards' supervisors had probably received some grease money for permitting it, so they were looking out for their supervisors in turn.

The two illegal hawkers, who were barely teenagers, were selling equipment cases, which one of them carried in a large net on his back.

As soon as his friend got to talk to a potential customer, he spread out a small folder which displayed all the different types of cases they had for sale.

On Tina's other side, an entire family—a father, mother and five children and a grandmother and another man who might have been an employee or an uncle—had spread out on the floor with all of their belongings. They had so much stuff that they took up a whole row of seats and the floor surrounding them. The children were tired, and one of the little ones was asleep on the floor.

Tina remembered this room well. She remembered the stink of despair of it, of the despair of not knowing whether you could stay or had to go, not knowing whether you would get a permit, and the despair of other people trying to sell cheap things just so that they could make ends meet.

Tina usually kept out of the way of these people because she was alone, and because ship owners were considered to be privileged citizens. News travelled fast in these stations, and Tina hated people accosting her because they thought she had money.

Tina's turn at the counter came when neither of the merchants nor the family with all the children had been seen yet. They had been there for much longer than she had, and it looked like they would be there for quite a while still. She felt guilty about that.

She crossed the large room to the counter at the far end, now remembering how close together these booths were, and how much you could hear what the person next to you was talking about. Some of those conversations were disturbingly private as well.

A merchant was discussing expenses and fees. He had a document open on his pad which showed lines of figures, and pointed to various ones. "See, and then I paid for this here and this is the order number and payment ID, and then you charge me twice here."

Seriously, she did not need to know all that.

The young man behind the counter looked far too young to be in this position. But then again, people who worked in the Port Authority customer relations office did not last very long.

He asked, "How can I help you?"

"I'd like to get an access code for my ship."

He asked for the model and registration.

He looked on the screen, and then raised his eyebrows.

"I can't see it here. When did you arrive here?"

"About fifteen years ago?"

His eyebrows went up further. "Oh. Then I'll need to look in a different part of the system. Hang on."

There were a number of moments of silence while he

looked, and then his face cleared. "I have it. You're lucky. The Property Retrieval Authority was about to sell it off."

"They would need my permission to do so." But the Property Retrieval Authority was a powerful body. They found ways to disown people if stuff took up too much space.

"Frankly, there are more outstanding fees on the ship then the old boat is worth."

"Wouldn't I be the one making the decision about how much it's worth?"

"Ultimately, yes, if we can locate you. But several notices have been sent out about fees in arrears, and none of the fees have been paid, at least in the past five years as far as I can track back. Everything owing on the ship has been archived. We'll release the ship once the fees have been paid, or I can arrange a sale for you."

"I don't think that will be necessary."

Hang on. She had paid fees. "What about the payments I made every year?"

"Yes, I can see them here, but they were nowhere near enough to cover the true cost of the berth."

"Then why didn't I receive notice about any fee increases?"

"That's what I am telling you. We sent notices, but none of them appear to have received a reply."

"Where did you send them?"

"To this address." He showed her the screen.

Oh what the hell. They had been sending the notices to Dexter because she'd used an account or address related to the Force to pay for the ship, or as administrative contact, and back then *it* still showed them as married. And by the usual administrative incompetence, no one had ever noticed that she wasn't getting those messages.

And Dexter, being her ex-husband, would just have laughed about them and put them aside, waiting until she got into trouble over it.

Anger built inside her. The vindictive old bastard. "Well then. Show me what I have to pay. I need the ship."

Again he turned the screen to her, and she nearly fainted. "Ten thousand credits?"

"There is a full itemised list of all the charges. They include all maintenance and cleaning fees, power—"

"I never use any power. I haven't used the ship for many years."

"We were never told to shut off the power."

"But I never used any. You can check that."

He looked. "Oh. I see."

"I shouldn't be charged for power. I want that taken off the bill. That would make a big difference."

"Only about four thousand."

"That's big enough for me. Take it off."

"I don't have authority to make those decisions. You would have to discuss that with my supervisor."

Tina balled her fists. There was no point getting angry at this young pipsqueak, because none of this was his fault.

He went out the back and returned a moment later with a woman with a stern face. She merely nodded to Tina, and listened as the young employee explained and asked how to deal with removal of an "abandoned" ship from the scrap queue.

"We'd have to move it into a docking port. I don't know how long it would take to find someone to pilot it."

Tina began, "I can fly—"

"No. Not around our facility, you won't. Not in a ship that

has not been inspected or accredited for fifteen years. We don't even know if it works."

"But surely it works. You moved the ship into this storage area. I left it in a docking port. It was in full working order."

"It's still at the same docking port, but the facility has grown around it. Getting it out will be a delicate operation which we can commence when we've received full payment of all outstanding fees."

"Can I at least have access to it so that I can start preparing it for sale?"

She gave Tina a suspicious look.

"That's the reason I'm here: to sell it."

"We can sell it for you."

"I want to sell it myself."

"Do you have any prospective buyers?"

"I think so." Optimistic, but whatever. It was none of the authority's business how and where she intended to sell, or for how much.

"Understand that you won't get a flight permit before that time."

"I understand. I don't want to fly it. I want to clear it out and get rid of the cobwebs and dust. Someone else can fly it."

With some negotiating, and the payment of three and a half thousand credits, she agreed that Tina could have access to the ship, only to clean it out, and explicitly not to fly it.

CHAPTER NINETEEN

TINA WENT BACK to the accommodation via the bank where she secured just enough funding to keep the authority happy. She was hoping that her objection to the unfair fees would be handled soon. There was the accommodation bill coming up as well.

This was getting ridiculous. Was that young man really suggesting that the ship was worth only ten thousand? He knew nothing about ships. Finn had said she'd be able to get a good price. He was an engineer. She trusted him.

When she got back to the hotel, Rex was sitting outside with a group of men a couple of years older than himself. They were laughing and talking, and Tina was happy at least that he hadn't been sulking in his room. She went to get some coffee at the counter and joined them.

The talk around the table was all about equipment. The men were in the fleet, and they were showing Rex all the latest in their technology.

He looked so much like a country boy. That harness he was wearing, though perfectly serviceable and sturdy, looked old-fashioned and a bit sad. At home in Dickson's Creek, she would never have noticed how dusty and worn it was, because everything there was dusty and worn.

But Rex obviously had an interest in technology, and she knew how important it was to him. It allowed him to get around and mingle with people in spaces that weren't about his disability.

She listened to their discussion while gulping down her coffee. It was hot and near-tasteless, but she needed it.

Rex finally turned to her. "Oh, hello Mum. Got the ship?"

It was such an innocent question. Tina didn't want to answer it with a cranky reply about leeches and rip-offs, but she was highly tempted. "I'm working on it. Come. We've got work to do."

One of the female recruits looked up at Rex. "You're leaving us? What a pity."

"You gotta do what the boss says," said a young man.

Rex got up from the table, which merely involved straightening his legs. He had pushed the chair away because he didn't need it. He followed Tina into the hallway with the usual zooming and clicking noises.

"Who are they?" Tina asked when they turned into the corridor to their room.

"Just some people who came to share my table, like yesterday with Finn. It was really busy and there was nowhere else for them to sit. They were very friendly."

"What were you talking about?"

"Just some things."

Definitely evasive. "Were they military crew from one of the Federacy ships?"

"Yeah. They were telling me all about the Force and about all the things they do as part of their jobs."

They walked silently for a bit and then he asked, "Do you think I would be able to join the Federacy Force?"

What? "You?" No.

"I like the things that those people told me they're doing. It's all electronics and equipment. I could do that."

The thought of Rex going to space clamped a hand around her heart. She'd protected her little boy. Who would help him in and out of his harness? How would he cope with the mandatory exercises? What would he do when people were nasty to him? "Did you ask them if you could join?"

"No. They said I should."

Now she understood the chain of events. They'd probably asked him what he did on Cayelle and he'd said he was bored, because that was what he always said. And then they'd said he could join the Force, whether they meant it or not. "It would be hard."

"With me being the way I am? You're allowed to say it."

"Can you just stop it for once?"

"But that's what you were going to say, right?"

"Actually, I wasn't. It's hard for everyone."

"I don't believe you."

"It is. I was eighteen when I joined. Those bastards take in the recruits and spend the next *year* making you feel as miserable as possible to get you to leave again."

"I doubt that. They're new recruits. They want people, right? They're advertising for people. I've seen the ads at Cayelle."

"What the PR department says is very different from reality. They only want people who are committed. It's not easy to be in the Force. It's boring. It's cramped. Sometimes rations are low. Usually, they're monotonous. The work is hard. Your colleagues can be nice, but they can also be extremely annoying. You're away from home for years and you never hear from your family—"

She had to stop talking. The memories were too painful. Her ship had pulled into a station—she didn't remember which—when the communications officer had taken her aside. On a grainy vid, her mother had informed her that her father had suddenly passed away. She'd missed his short illness and the funeral. Next time she went home, there was a massive hole where he used to be. She could see him in the shed whittling away at a woodwork project. She could see him in the garden dragging the hoses. She offered her mother to take leave for a year, but her mother had gotten word that she had been offered a position at the Perseus Agency, a job she knew Tina coveted, and had hated the thought that her daughter would give that up and then blame her old mother for missing the opportunity.

For what? The agency had used her and spat her out. She couldn't stand the thought of her little baby going through that.

Rex met her eyes. He was young and didn't understand any of that. When she objected to something, he thought it was always about him and his disabilities, and they would have a long argument about it. She was tired of it.

"If you want to go after you finish school and have your certificate, I can't stop you. I can only tell you what my experience has been."

"And you think it will be too hard for me?"

He met her eyes, and she couldn't bring herself to say yes. She didn't even know if she was right. Nor did he know that she was afraid he would learn a tough lesson. Maybe she was even more afraid he would do well, and she would be left on the sidelines, cheering him on from a very long distance.

That was it. *She* would be left. This was not about Rex. It was about her.

She shrugged, because there were no words that seemed right.

Rex continued, "I thought because we have no money for an exoskeleton—no, don't say anything. I *know* we have no money and I'm not arguing about it—I could work and pay for it myself. The man I was talking to said that the Force employs people who wear harnesses all the time and that the Force has payment plans for them."

"I'd hate for you to sign up just so that you can get an exoskeleton. I'll look at it when you finish school. I mean it. By that time, we should be able to afford it. I've budgeted for it."

He met her eyes again, knowing full well that if she used the money from selling the ship to pay off the owner, they couldn't afford it, not if they also needed to eat, and it didn't seem that would change any time soon.

She didn't want him to join the Force. She wanted to spare him all the pain that she had suffered. The betrayal, the bypassing, the mocking, the bullying. The gradual hollowing out of her confidence. All because she didn't agree with the direction the agency was taking.

No. Surely there had to be better places for him to work.

But a voice in the back of her mind said, *You haven't really put much effort into giving him options, have you?*

And she knew how true that was, that she couldn't expect him to want to look after a dusty shop in a dusty corner of a dusty planet and watch over all her dusty cactuses when she was gone. "You're fifteen. We'll talk about this once you have your senior school certificate."

"It's not about that."

"Yes, it is. They only take people with good marks. So you better start studying."

She didn't know that bit for sure, but hopefully, he'd have forgotten about joining the Force by the time he finished school. And by the time she had done a better job giving him interesting choices for his future. If Jake thought she could work for his company while living at Dickson's Creek, surely Rex could find some part of technology to produce or program that would make him money. She would buy him computers and scanners and 3D printers and whatever he needed.

She changed the subject. "Well, I got the keys to the ship, even if they wouldn't give me a permit to fly it yet, but we can get started on cleaning it up so that I can put it up for sale."

They entered their room, and Tina retrieved the small bag that she had prepared with all the items that she might need. It included keys to the cupboards, controls and flight devices, but, in honesty, she should have packed a couple of mops and cloths to clean, because it would probably be pretty dusty inside. They would have to go past the shops and buy them.

Rex asked, "What's wrong?"

Tina walked past him to the door.

"I asked you something."

"I'll sort it out."

But she was not two steps into the hallway, when he said, "We are here together. I can help you sort things out."

Tina didn't really think that he could, but already he had changed so much that she should at least discuss it. "I'm just a bit cranky, because everything and everybody here is charging me money. They wouldn't release the ship until I paid up all the fees over the last fifteen years that haven't been paid. They came to quite a bit, and they sent all the reminders to your father. So I never got them."

"He didn't send them to you?"

That would've been the normal thing to do. But Dexter was never known to be considerate. On the other hand she had sworn not to go into the politics of their marriage in front of Rex. After all, Dexter had never even seen the boy.

"I've appealed against those fees, especially the electricity charges. I was never here and never used any. They could see that and are considering it. They gave me access to the ship. I have the code. I want to get started as soon as possible. This place is costing me an arm and a leg, and I'm nervous about that."

CHAPTER TWENTY

TINA AND REX made their way through the maze of corridors of the station to the docking areas. First, they came to the modern main hall, a hive of activity with people going in all directions to the docking berths. Each section had a number. A lot of tourists with luggage stood crammed in front of the Sector 3 lift. Only a handful of military officers waited in front of the Sector 2 lift.

Tina and Rex got into the lift to the A sector, where no one else was waiting.

The lift took them through the weightless centre of the station.

The door opened into a much older hall with dated creamy yellow lino on the floor. It was not nearly as busy as in the first hall, or, for that matter, all the rest of the station. Next they needed to find the way to number 614.

They walked through the passage, Rex's heavy steps thudding on the metal floor. As they went, the tubes grew narrower, and the structures older. Tina tried very hard to remember this from when she had come here but could not. She only remembered how down and exhausted she had felt. She remembered going into the Port Authority office, but little else.

"It looks like no one's been here for ages," Rex said.

Yes, it felt like the ships behind the access tubes had been dead for years, a kind of lost-and-found collection in space. "This is the way they build these space ports," Tina said. "They insert the new sections of the port in between the body of the station and the docking port's extension arms, which means they just let out the walkways further."

She was trying to sound upbeat, but she was beginning to have a very bad feeling about this. This area of the station looked downright abandoned. The floor felt dusty underfoot. People had scrawled on the walls. Not all of the lights worked. Here and there were signs that people lived here, people with no homes, who had piled all their possessions into little heaps of tattered clothes and discarded boxes.

Homeless people were a problem in the civilian stations. When you were cast out of a ship, had no work and no money, and no ID, what else could you do?

"Here. I think this is it." The number on the side of the docking tube entrance matched the number on her access key: 614. If the Port Authority woman was to be believed, this was the spot she had left the ship, and it hadn't been moved for fifteen years. The port had simply grown around it.

The access tube was short but shrouded in semidarkness. A light switch on the side of the tube didn't work.

The door at the end was closed. A control panel beside the door was turned off. There were signs that the door had been forced open, with the area around the lock damaged.

Her heart sank. "Somebody has gotten in before us."

Why had she gone through the effort of paying that much money if some person could just get in? It would be scandalous if, for the money they charged, the Port Authority didn't even make an effort to keep the ship safe, or to keep on the power that they charged her for.

Maybe she should take the ship out in protest. Cut off the cables and leave.

But it would need to be refuelled. Also, flying the ship out and detaching it from the station would bring out all kinds of people with weapons. Better play by the rules.

When she tried the access code that the Port Authority had given her, the door only opened half the distance, revealing the ship's dark interior. "It's jammed."

And that meant Rex couldn't get in with his harness. "Wait here. I'm going to have a look to see if I can open the door fully from the inside."

Tina squeezed sideways through the opening, wondering whether Rex would be able to get in at all. She didn't remember the accessway being this narrow, and she imagined docking the cargo bay would be another fee on top of the one she had already paid as well as embarrassing for him.

It was very dark inside the cabin of the ship. It smelled of... staleness, like the contents of a bag of clothes that you hadn't worn for many years. There was also a faint scent of cold food.

Phooey. A good cleanout was definitely in order.

That smell of food worried her. It was probably why the door had shown signs of having been forced open. She looked around in the darkness. No one was in here right now, were they?

"Are you all right?" Rex asked from the door.

She could see his silhouette backlit by the light in the passage. "I think so," she said. Where was the light switch in here again?

The control console, the emergency lights and projection screens that would normally provide a low level of ambient light in the cabin were off. But a tiny light was on at the far end of the control panel, and by its glow, Tina could see the familiar benches and tables and a cupboard that held equipment, and the navigation module and the pilot's seat.

Memories flowed back to her.

A soft sound came out of the darkness.

Tina froze and listened. That had been much closer than the groans of the station constantly moving, the clicking of expanding and contracting metal and the clanging of ships docking. "Hello, is anyone here?"

She stood still for a while, but heard no further noise. So she crossed the cabin and turned on the light. True to his word, the young man had restored the power to the vessel.

But my, it was such a mess in the cabin. Apart from layers of dust, she saw clear signs that someone had lived here at some stage. Tattered and dirty blankets lay in a heap on the floor. Someone had been using the couch as a bed, and discarded food containers stood on the table. Those looked fairly recent.

Again, she heard a noise.

"Who's there?" she repeated. "I am the owner of the ship. If you are here unlawfully, please come out. I won't do anything to you, but you will have to leave."

Again, she got no reply, but she still sensed someone here. So she went to the sleeping cabin door, and opened it.

An avalanche of rubbish cascaded over her feet: boxes, bottles, broken equipment, dirty rags.

Tina swore, and Rex, who was looking in through the door said, "Are you all right?"

"Someone has used this to store rubbish." Obviously she would not find anyone in here.

The next door was a panel that slid aside and that, in flight, would fold out into a tube that led to the habitat module, attached to the bottom of a tube that swung around to create a semblance of gravity. When in dock, that tube was stowed, so there was no space behind the panel.

So she opened the door to the cargo bay. She turned on the light and was met with an explosion of squawking, honking and flapping.

Two large and furious balls of orange feet, beaks and feathers rushed towards her.

Tina slammed the door shut and leaned with her back against it, while the door was being attacked from the other side with much honking and hissing.

"What was that?" Rex asked.

"Geese." Seriously, who was keeping geese in her cargo hold? She waited until the animals calmed down.

The cupboards on the right hand side of the hallway held space suit liners and other supplies. The hard suits themselves—if they hadn't been removed—would be in the hold with the geese. But Tina guessed the suits would be gone, sold off to whoever had paid the most money for them.

She went back into the cabin, and realised there was one place she forgot to check out: the navigation bay. And she remembered that in the navigation bay was a hatch that provided access to the engine compartment, at least to the part accessible during flight. It was a tiny cubbyhole with, at the bottom of a narrow ladder, a number of panels for fine-tuning the engine and other ship processes. The room was not big enough to sleep in, but would be perfect for hiding. She yanked the hatch up, and shone a light inside.

It hit the face of a girl.

She was in her early teenage years, very skinny, with skin so pale it seemed translucent, and with dirty short hair that was coarsely hacked off close to her head.

She screamed and held her hands above her head.

"Whoa, whoa. Don't panic. I'm not going to eat you."

"Please, please, don't hit me!"

"Calm down."

"Don't hit me. Don't hit me. I will pay."

"Shut up!"

"Don't hit meeeee!"

"Did you hear what I said? Shut up."

The girl fell quiet. She glanced through the gap between her arms.

"See? I won't harm you. Now come out, and then take your animals and leave the ship."

"Please, I have nowhere else to go."

"I need the ship. It's mine, and I think you broke into it."

"Please, please?"

"Is that the only thing you can say? What is your name?"

Tina had to repeat the question three times before the girl lowered her arms, uncovering her face. She was a mousey, skinny thing with huge eyes. Her pale skin was marked with red rashes from her chin down. Her arms were thin as sticks. One of them bore a black tattoo of a rune-like mark.

She looked like a child, but her budding breasts made her about the same age as Rex.

"See? We don't bite. What's your name?"

"Rasa."

"How old are you? Where are your parents?"

"I'm fifteen. My ma didn't want me because her boyfriend didn't like me, so she left me here."

"Did you come here on a ship?"

She nodded.

"Where did you come from?"

"I don't know. My ma is crazy and never told me. We lived on ships that went around until she decided she had enough of me."

"When was that?"

"When I was ten."

"And you've lived here ever since?"

"Yes. I wanted to find my brother."

Tina wondered how in the world she survived for all that time. "Well, Rasa, you can't stay here. I'm sure there are a lot of other places in the station where you can set up your cubby. Just get out now, and I won't tell anyone that you were here." She reached into her pack, and retrieved the packet she had brought for lunch. "Here, you can have this. Just take your things and animals and leave."

The girl climbed out of the cubby, took Tina's offer, gathered up a blanket but not the other things, and left for the cargo hold. When she opened the door, the geese waddled out, still honking indignantly.

There were five of them, big and white, huddled together with their heads held up high, regarding Tina with their beady eyes.

Rasa herded the animals through the cabin.

She had to walk past Rex at the entrance, and she took a step back and shuffled against the wall.

"He doesn't bite, you know."

The girl continued very carefully, eyes wide and fixed on Rex, until she was past him, and then she ran into the passage and disappeared around the corner. The geese waddled after her.

"What was all that about?" Rex asked.

"I'm not sure. Some kind of squatter."

"What does the ship look like?"

"I haven't looked at the vitals yet." Tina turned back to the pilot's seat.

When she sat down, her mind went many years into the past. When she had last come here, she had been broken and tired. After flying a long way from Pandana, she had been on the ship alone, and that was not ideal because you had to sleep sometimes.

She remembered how glad she had felt when the ship was safely in dock, and how much she wanted to leave that world behind. She had put the ship up for sale at first, but she had received one laughable offer, so she decided to keep it in dock, and go down to the planet to have some time to think.

Who would have expected how quickly that time would grow into fifteen years?

She'd discovered she was pregnant while staying in a dingy hotel in Peris City, and she'd gone through a pregnancy marred with health issues. Rex was born in a clinic in Peris City. Tina still remembered the horrified look on the nurse's face.

She brushed the dust off the control panels. It was a bit more than dust, too, because her hand came away black from some kind of mould that grew on all the walls.

She reached for the compartment that held the

earpieces, found one still inside and attached it to her ear. Then she turned the main switch on.

A familiar humming sound went through the craft. The lights on the control panels flickered into life. The screen in front of her said two percent charged.

Well, she couldn't expect any better than that.

She tested the radio. An automated voice in her ear said, "Kelso Station Control. State your intentions."

That worked.

She turned on the radar and navigation, which also appeared to be working, although she would definitely want to subject the system to some tests before declaring it safe to fly.

She turned on the on-board AI. A male voice sounded through the cabin. "Hello there, this is Benny. I hope you're having a wonderful time. How can I help you?"

Tina cringed. She forgot she'd installed that swanky voice. She replied in military curtness, "Check status."

Benny was silent for a bit, and then he said, "Oh dearie me, I have many updates that need to be installed and will need thirty-two hours to do that. Until that time, my function shall be quite impaired. Do you want me to go ahead?"

"Yes."

"Mum, who are you talking to?" Rex asked at the door.

"Just the onboard AI." She needed to change his voice to something less embarrassing.

"Oh. He sounded like some playboy."

"I'll update him."

To be honest, she was surprised that the system started up at all. At least it looked like she had a functioning ship which, frankly, was more than she had expected. "We'll spend a few days cleaning this all up and getting rid of all this rubbish, and then we'll be fine."

"We?" Rex said from near the door.

"You can help if you want."

"I can't get through the door."

And that was another problem.

CHAPTER TWENTY-ONE

SHE KNEW ONLY one way to solve the problem of getting Rex into the ship: she needed to take his harness apart and reassemble it inside.

She retrieved a blanket from inside and spread it out on the floor. Then she helped Rex onto it, and took off his arms and legs.

The body of the harness needed to come off, too, because with it, he was too heavy for her to carry.

While all this was happening, a number of homeless urchins came a bit further down the passage to watch while Tina took off the protective swaddling around the bottom of his body.

Rex didn't like that.

"They're laughing at me," he said, lifting his head to glare at them.

"Just lie still, and I can do this quickly."

"I'm ridiculous. I look like a baby."

Tina rolled him in a blanket, a sorry stump of a human being, just a body with a head.

She carried him into the ship, and when she came back for the harness found that two of the young urchins were looking at it.

"Scoot," she said, flapping her hand.

The boys took a few steps back, but she wasn't sure if they understood.

She picked up one half of the harness, noticing by the harsh light how worn some of the joints were.

She removed his pad and emptied the container into it and wrapped up the sides. She carried the resulting heavy parcel to the nearby recycling chute, enveloped by the associated smell.

The boys giggled. "Does he, like, poo in there as well?" one asked.

The other boy chuckled. "Like a baby."

"He's much bigger than a baby."

"What would you do if you were born without arms or legs?" Tina snapped at them.

"I'd be dead, miss. I got no one to get me one of those walker things."

"Well, then, don't laugh at other people. Go somewhere else. Scoot."

While she walked back to the ship's entrance, one of the boys elbowed another in the side. That boy, easily the youngest in the group, came forward. "Miss, if you have a moment."

"No, I don't."

"We can work for you, if you need any help."

"That's a bit rich, after insulting my son. I suggest you take yourself off somewhere else and stop bothering us."

The boy retreated. He looked disappointed.

She watched until the group had walked so far down the walkway that they disappeared around the curve.

She carried the other half of Rex's harness inside, refreshed all the pads inside, attached the empty container, and lifted Rex back into the harness. Once he was in, he checked that everything was working, and walked a couple of lumbering paces up and down the hall.

It was barely wide enough for him, and he wouldn't fit in any of the cabins.

Anyway, they could get started.

Tina went back outside in the hallway, filled a bucket with water, and put in some of the soap that she had bought. She set up Rex to clean the walls and floors and sweep the dust off the seats. He found a complete stash of squirrelled-away canteen supplies in one of the cupboards, as well as a blanket and some spare clothes.

"Do you think that girl was living here?" he said.

"Yes, she was. That's what people do when they don't have a home."

"What do you mean—don't have a home?"

"Not everyone is lucky enough that they can afford a place to live."

He frowned. "That means she has no family to look after her?"

"Some people don't. It sounded like she ran away from an abusive stepfather."

His face looked disturbed. "Then we just kicked her out of her home."

"She'll find another place."

"I don't like those boys outside. They look like they could cause trouble for a girl by herself."

"Oh, urchins are used to that sort of thing. They know how to keep themselves safe."

But Rex, in his usual innocence, managed to penetrate a corner that made her uneasy. Station authorities were rarely kind to these abandoned children. She had heard stories that they regularly rounded up all of them and forced them to undergo radiation that made them infertile. Authorities said they did it to prevent misery, but it also rendered the girls suitable as sex slaves that could be abused and traded with impunity.

Who knew what abuse the girl Rasa had fled? The tattoo on her arm might be a mark of previous ownership.

And now she was thinking about this poor girl instead of her own problems of having to sell the ship and getting the money so that she and Rex could survive.

And yes, Rex was right about it, but what could she do? She couldn't be responsible for the survival of the entire human race. She had a hard enough time looking after her own survival.

Rex was occupied cleaning, and while Benny's updates were running she might as well have a look for any information that hadn't been on the ship's systems when she left it. She checked all the system's folders and data storage, but found little that shouldn't be there.

She did find a statement of her previous finances, which included her retirement allowance and what the Force called an "Exit package". The retirement allowance was still in an account somewhere. She was only allowed to take it out at the age of sixty and that was a decent while off yet. The exit package was partially still in the account. She had only withdrawn two thousand credits of it—to visit the planet—and had been unable to access her account from Gandama because the bank staff were just too incompetent.

A bit less then eight thousand was left over.

That money was hers and would go a distance towards paying the hotel so she didn't have to put it on credit to be sorted out later.

She noticed Rex looking over her shoulder.

"Anything important?" he asked.

"A bit of money. Not terribly much, but it will help, if I can get it out."

He frowned. "Who's Alethia?" He sounded suspicious, in a don't-tell-me-I-have-another-sister way.

"Alethia means truth in old Greek. It's the name of the ship."

"Oh." He gave her a sheepish look. "Did you name it?"

"No. Ships are registered with their name. It's part of their registration. It takes a lot of effort to change it."

But she had liked the ship's name a lot. The truth. That's what she was going to tell.

When she left, she had taken all the sensitive documents and had left them in a document box on Kelso, with a note for someone from the agency to pick them up. She wondered if the agency had ever retrieved it.

She wondered...

Every time Agency personnel went on a mission in civilian space, they received three fake identities, in case they needed to stay undercover or use any of these boxes. They would designate one identity as the one allowed to pick up the box's contents. This identity could be used by other people and would be destroyed afterwards.

Tina checked in the general population database, and

there was still a person called Louise Metvier. The other identities also remained intact.

It didn't look like the identity had been used. That could only mean no one had touched her data. And that could only be because someone—Dexter—would have kept her information from reaching civilised space.

Why? Was it only because he feared missing his performance indicators? That seemed a dumb reason.

Maybe she should check and take her documents out and forward them to the Federacy Force command some other way. It was probably too late, but at least she would have done the right thing.

Another item on the to-do list.

While she wiped down the control console and kept an eye on the status of the system scan, her thoughts went to her work with the project.

When she had arrived, the retiring biologist had shown her the secret of the project: a tear in the fabric of space that the small station had already been researching for a few decades, very carefully and with great secrecy. A tear in the fabric of space meant something was on the other side, and those old scientists were keenly aware of the danger that this other side might pose when exposed to the human universe.

The area showed up brightly in most frequencies. But it was small, and space was bent around the tear such that bodies—like planets, moons, and space stations—wouldn't be sucked into it. They'd thought it was a mini black hole but, when they developed telescopes that penetrated the barrier, they found it wasn't.

Tina had come onto the project to look at strange phenomena in plants grown at the station in experiments and for consumption by the crew. She had found evidence of interference by alien life, which wasn't uncommon, but was trying to trace it, when a cloud of dust exploded from the tear.

It could only mean that there was pressure, something on the other side. Another universe? A wormhole?

She had wanted to report it, to warn everyone of any potential danger. The cloud had lingered in space for about an hour until it had dispersed so much that she could no longer see it. Whatever it was, those particles were alien and dangerous and the project should withdraw.

The project's command, a hardline officer by the name of Bartlett, had wanted to hear none of it, because he had his own productivity goals in mind. The Force's upper command had been questioning the need to have the station, because they hadn't produced anything useful in over thirty years. He thought they could use some of their other discoveries, because...who knew? Dexter had defended him, and Tina had not been able to make him understand the danger. The relationship had already been frosty, but that argument just blew it out of the water.

Rex was talking to someone at the door.

"What's going on?" Tina asked.

"They want to know if you want to purchase cleaning services," he said.

"They? Who is it?"

"Some company. They're wearing all the same shirts."

"Can't they see we're doing it ourselves?"

A voice came from outside, and a young man said, "We can clean your ship so that it looks new, so that you can get the best possible price when you list it for sale."

"Thank you very much, but we are not selling. Please leave us alone."

The young men retreated, and Rex looked at her, surprised. "We are not selling?"

"Of course we are, but I have no idea how he knows this, which means someone must have told him. Hopefully now he thinks he's got the wrong ship and they'll stay away."

Rex's frown deepened. "Do you think someone is watching us?"

"I am certain of it." Who or why remained a question. She just hoped that they wouldn't get any bolder than this. First Finn, who knew who she was, then the men who followed her, then she happened to run into Jake and his insistence she work for him, then the urchin in the ship, and now this.

The rest of the day was spent scrubbing, wiping and turning the tired dusty-looking vessel into something a little bit more respectable.

Slowly, the smell of disuse vanished, too.

Benny came back online, and Tina let Rex have some time with him by giving him the task to copy all the financial stuff and erase it from the ship's systems. Whenever she walked past, Rex would be laughing. Benny really was hilarious. She pitied the new owner to have to deal with Benny's extensive knowledge of swear words.

But then Rex surprised her by saying, "Mum, do you know that you can get from this onboard AI into the dock-side computers?"

She didn't believe him but, when she looked over his shoulder, found it to be true. The screen in front of him displayed all kinds of information about the ship that should not be available to them, including options to turn on and off communication and power. They worked, too.

"How did you do that?" Tina asked him.

"When you go into the AI's control module, there is an option for *base umbilicals control* and when you go there, it connects with the dockside computer. It looks like it's a menu that the ship defaults to because the original control modules were superseded and the ship's onboard AI is not ready to handle those."

"How do you know all that?"

"From all my *unreliable* friends all over the Federacy."

"You talk about getting into computer systems?"

"They talk about that a lot, because they have nothing else to talk about. It's not like we can talk about girls or going out."

That was kind of disturbing. She didn't like snooping on Rex and the online communities he was in, but if she'd known that some of them were hackers, she might have told him to be careful—which would have had exactly the opposite of the desired effect.

At the end of the day, she went through the reverse process of taking Rex out of the harness and carrying him and the pieces through the door separately.

Fortunately, this time there were no urchins or other people to bother them; but a lone security officer walked past, raising his eyebrows at her.

He said, "Hmm. An owner turning up to retrieve their possessions doesn't happen often."

"It's a fully functional ship. This is a docking port. The ship will fly out of the dock."

"Good luck with that. The Property Retrieval Authority loves getting rid of things." He laughed and continued on his patrol.

That had been the bane of commercial stations even when she was in the Force. Sooner or later, even the most well-organised station turned into a graveyard for abandoned and superseded junk that no one came to pick up but that no one could legally dispose of, either because the owners couldn't be contacted or because they had put in place protections that didn't allow the station to seize the property and sell it off.

That was what the Property Retrieval Authority did. Study like a hawk when those protections expired. She had just barely rescued the ship from their fingers.

CHAPTER TWENTY-TWO

"YOU GO AHEAD," Tina said to Rex when they arrived at the start of the commercial passage. They had navigated back to the lift, into the central docking hall and through the maze of passages that led to the commercial area. Shops lined both sides of the passage, the accommodation was at the end, and there was not much that Rex could do except linger at the shops. She should trust him a bit more not to make every possible mistake.

He frowned at her. "What are you going to do?"

"I'm going to the Station Storage Office to check if I left anything in a locker on the station. It's not very interesting and I won't be long. I'll meet you back at the hotel. Feel free to look around. Just don't spend any money."

"Oh. All right." He smiled.

In reality, she wasn't allowed to take a second person to the agency locker. She might not work there anymore, and the locker might have been abandoned, but she'd adhere to protocol.

She watched Rex on his way back to the accommodation and then set off.

A quick ride in the elevator to the next level brought her to another busy passage, this one with all the business offices and things like medical practices.

Most of the citizens who lived at Kelso were either employed in closed-system agriculture or rare-earth mining from asteroids. As with any station, many also provided services for the people living at the station or the visiting ships.

Civilian stations also attracted a fair amount of illegal activity.

Ahead in the corridor a number of people hung around in small groups—not the type of people that Tina would voluntarily engage with. Most were quite young, shabbily dressed, and sported a varying number of things that could be used as weapons.

The use of guns and knives was prohibited by any except authorised people, but gangs had taken to carrying things like clubs and belts studded with metal. Any of those could be used as a weapon.

She walked in between the groups, ignoring them. None of them paid her any attention. And then she realised that they were all standing in front of the place she was going.

The Station Storage Office was on the left-hand side, an empty shopfront with just a counter and a number of screens.

She went inside. She didn't need to speak to the single attendant behind the counter. He looked busy, handing someone a box from which all manner of items protruded.

The group of young people in the corner watched this

interaction, and as soon as the box's owner made his way to the exit, they approached him.

Tina was too far away to hear what was being said, but she saw how the owner shook his head and then the man's female partner yelled something at the young men, at which everyone in the room looked around.

"Any trouble?" the man behind the desk asked.

"No. These people were just about to leave us alone," the woman said.

The man behind the counter glared at the group of youths, who quickly made their way out of the office.

Someone else in the room asked, "What time is the auction?"

A mate chimed in. "You're already late. We're waiting."

"We shall start momentarily," the man behind the counter said, and then he spotted Tina and asked, "Can I help you?" Almost as if he was glad for a distraction.

"No, I'm just looking something up."

Tina went to one of the screens, but the tension in the room could be cut with a knife.

The office's public access screens were placed on the four sides of pillars that supported the roof. There was plenty of room around them, and instructions were written in large script on the main menu. *Enter your name, and the date that your items entered storage.*

Tina was about to type in any of the names she would have used as aliases—fake IDs with proper identification if this was needed—but then she stopped.

All these people could see over her shoulder.

So she went to another screen, one on the far side of the pillar, where no one could stand behind her.

But people still watched, and more people came into the

shop. The employee opened a door to another room which contained rows of chairs. It seemed the auction was about to begin.

Most of the young people filed in, but some lingered back, as if hesitant to be seen in the auction room.

From what Tina remembered, there was usually a lively trade in selling keys and unknown content of lockers, including bidding wars for those keys, especially if they were *virgin keys*, meaning that no one had opened the locker since it had become legal for the station authority to confiscate it.

Tina typed in the name of the contact she'd keyed to be able to pick up the content of the box: Louise Metvier. She selected the date she had deposited the material in the box. Then she was prompted she to show her ID to the scanner at the top of the screen.

Tina pulled out her ID and held it up, mentally crossing her fingers that this fifteen-year-old process still worked.

The computer opened an information screen.

The locker was in the document storage area, and the screen gave her a number as well as a code that she needed to open the locker. Tina copied it down, and then exited the screen after having given the command that the data should be destroyed after she had retrieved the content.

She quickly left the office.

She found her locker in a section that had a wall with tiny cubicles labelled for document storage. It was easy to find, but she walked around the area twice just to make sure no one was following her.

Of course no one stored actual documents in these boxes, just devices that held the documents. It was one of the few ways to ensure that no one hacked the information.

It was such a device that Tina found inside the small

space: a small reader of a generic make, a dark-grey flat box that would project its contents either on a table or wall or a special screen, if you had one. In accordance with Perseus Agency rule, it was not linkable to wireless networks, and any copying had to be done with a dock or cable, the old-fashioned way.

There used to be a shelf in the office that contained boxes of these things for general use of agents.

This was the device that she had placed in here, untouched, because the seal over the screen was still intact.

To her surprise, the locker contained a second device, one she definitely hadn't put in there. It, too, was dark-grey and flat, sealed with a piece of tape. She guessed it to be a few years more recent.

Well, crap.

She took both out of the locker, stuck them in the pocket of her jacket and shut the door. Then she made her way down the corridor. Her footsteps echoed weirdly in the narrow space, creating the impression that someone was following her. She looked around, but the corridor on both sides was empty, although the curved floor did not allow her to see very far.

Without her uniform and her weapon she felt naked. Theft and robbery were quite common in these stations and police were always busy. Many of the big passenger ships arrived with stowaways who might work in the kitchens for their passage, but if discovered they would be left behind on the stations. They had no papers, no official identity and no home. Back when she worked with the agency, the captain would always warn the crew about them when the ship came into dock.

A few of these illegal ship people sat on the floor a bit

further down the passage. They barely looked up when Tina passed.

But as soon as she had gone a little distance, she noticed that a group of three men walked behind her. They pretended to be talking to each other, but they stopped whenever she did, and made a clear effort not to look in her direction when she looked in theirs.

They were not in uniform, and didn't have the typical slightly-too-casual appearance of Federacy agents trying to look casual.

No, they were just a bunch of friends going for a walk. Or were they? She was starting to see danger in everything.

Still, it was better to go back to the hotel.

Ahead in the corridor, a group of people were entering a door that, when she came closer, turned out to lead into a stairwell. She followed them down to the next level, walking quickly.

She stopped at the bottom of the stairs to see if the three men were still behind her.

They were.

Shit.

She let herself out of the door at the bottom of the stairwell, and entered another featureless corridor.

It was virtually empty, except for two people at the very end.

Tina headed that direction, but had not yet reached the end before the door to the stairs behind her opened and one of the men peeked out.

The fact that they were following her like this meant they were not just casual friends. They were also not from the station authorities, because the authorities had many other ways to follow people inside the station. They only needed to track people's communication devices.

These guys weren't even smart about following her.

Holy crap, what did they want? She had no way to defend herself. Rex was alone at the hotel.

Tina sped to the end of the corridor as fast as she dared without running. It ended in a T-intersection. She randomly chose left, because that was the direction the other people had gone. She had no idea where she was, and hoped that if she followed other people, she might end up in the commercial passage from where she could find her way back.

But the new corridor was just as long and featureless as the previous, and what was worse, no one was in it.

Tina ran.

She looked over her shoulder several times, but she knew that she was not fast enough to outrun a couple of men half her age, if they decided to give chase. She was woefully out of condition.

At that point, her training kicked in. When followed, and finding another safe area is not an option, do something unexpected.

The biggest unexpected thing she could do was to go back to the ship, anywhere that led these characters away from Rex.

The docks were well monitored with few people, and few ways to hide your face or identity scan from security cameras. It was a gamble, but all spies—whether from the Federacy or not—were reluctant to be identified. They might not follow her in there.

Then she could fake some sort of issue with the ship and call a security guard to escort her out. Or she could find something to keep in her pocket as weapon.

She quickly made her way through the passages back to the docks. The disks in her pocket thumped against her leg.

It seemed she had been right about the pursuers: they didn't dare come into the lift with her.

She had at least as much advantage on the men as it took the lift to get back. If they were going to follow at all.

When the door opened, Tina ran through the passage.

But when she arrived at the ship, it was to find someone already there.

CHAPTER TWENTY-THREE

IN THE ACCESS TUNNEL, someone had piled up blankets, and when Tina came closer, a goose waddled out of the shadows, honking at her.

"Lenna, come back here!" a young voice called.

The urchin Rasa rushed out and grabbed the goose around the neck and chest.

Then she stopped, looking at Tina. "Oh. It's you."

"I thought I said you couldn't stay in my ship."

"I'm not in the ship."

True. "But you're blocking the entrance."

"You can get past."

"Without getting bitten?"

"I'll keep them away. I swear." The goose in her arms was trying to free itself by pushing its orange feet against her shirt.

"Why did you come back?"

"I have nowhere else to go. Outside, this area all belongs to the gang. When I go there, they steal my food and hurt me and try to sell me to the pimps."

"What sort of gang is this?"

"Thugs, you know. They mug people and steal stuff from the big ships. They get caught sometimes, but then they come out of jail and join the gangs again. They're not nice to girls. If you're a girl, you want to stay away from them. They're all around the docks and that area."

"All right. Stay here. I still don't want the animals in the ship. I'm trying to sell it and need it cleaned up."

"You mean the ship will be taken away?"

"I don't know what the new owner will do with it."

Rasa's eyes were wide. Heavens. Just how long had she lived inside?

Tina had just kicked the girl out of a safe home and now she was going to take the home away.

Rasa held the geese to the side while Tina walked past to the ship's entrance.

She asked, "Do they lay eggs?"

"Of course they do. They're all girls. I can sell you eggs. They're very big. Half a credit for four."

"I'll keep that in mind."

Tina went inside the craft and sat down on the bench, leaning her head in her hands. This was all a lot less easy than she had imagined. She'd come here simply to sell the ship, not to solve all the unsolvable problems she had left behind, and all of everyone else's problems, and save the universe while she was at it.

Ultimately, a desire to save humanity from itself was why she had left the Force, and, having found that, fifteen years later, humanity was still keen to destroy itself, all kinds of reasons were tugging at her to have a second attempt at saving the universe.

She blew out a breath.

Let's see what was on this extra disk that obviously someone at some stage managed to place in the locker.

An image of a man popped up in the air. He wore a Federacy Force uniform. He was middle-aged, his hair was short and grey, his eyes brown and his bearded face quite friendly. Well, damn it, that was Vasily Demetrov, colleague and friend.

He stood at the front of Project Charon Station's meeting room. Some of Tina's old colleagues sat in the audience. Even Jake Monterra was there.

Vasily was a doctor for the agency and, once a year, he would give a health report of all the agency's employees, as part of a very long and boring progress report.

"What we see here is the trend continuing from last year and the year before. We have an increasing number of our research workforce struck by a variety of health conditions that they didn't exhibit prior to joining the agency, and that they can't attribute to anything in particular, other than that their employment by the agency has been a common trigger."

Someone in the audience made a protest.

"Yes, I know about the objections that people voice against me, but the data doesn't lie. This is not a healthy place to work. When you join the agency's research staff, you are three times more likely than the general population to contract certain conditions. You are four times more likely to contract other conditions, and up to seven times more likely to contract an illness of any kind. This happens over so many different conditions that it can no longer be considered a statistical anomaly. Something in our environment at the station is making us ill."

The audience wanted to know more. Had he checked the

recycling and food production, had he considered sabotage by those groups who disliked the station where it was and who might have, by some means, obtained a pretty decent feel for their operations?

Vasily said they'd checked all this.

Tina remembered this talk, even if she couldn't see herself in the audience, and didn't remember anyone recording it.

Tina also remembered how, during this talk, she had the revelation that this could be caused by the dust from the rift. It should be something they should investigate.

She'd grown accustomed to seeing the flashes of light that erupted from the area known as "the mouth". She'd seen the chunks of rock that the agency pushed into it disappear. She'd done analyses on the fragments of material that the mouth spat out.

Biological analysis, no less. Then the material she'd spotted coming out reached the area where they sampled rocks. They found something: molecular structures that were dividing and growing as they were being observed in a solution and at a temperature where nothing should be alive. That was the point at which she had become concerned.

The projection changed to show herself in the spot where Vasily had stood.

"The existence of a rift at Project Charon is a poorly kept secret. It was discovered thirty years before I started working with the agency, when the agency was looking for an area to conduct antimatter experiments, but no one is sure if these experiments caused the rift, made it bigger or whether it was already there. At first no one knew what this rift was. We discovered it's a portal to another universe. We noticed that clouds of dust came out. We sampled the objects that came into contact with these clouds of particles. I was appointed to the team as biologist, but after the initial sampling, I was told my services were no longer needed. The only time I was allowed to study this material, I was highly concerned, but when I raised the alarm, authorities only told us to monitor the situation closely."

The younger Tina in the projection ran her hand through her hair. She looked pale and ill. Pregnant with Rex, even if she didn't know it at the time.

"We saw the molecular structures on our probes, but we never got to see data from any of the other samples they collected that had come out of the rift. I find the obstruction of the flow of data across research groups disturbing at the very least—let's not forget we're talking about alien organisms—but certain elements in the research division seem what I shall call "uninterested". So I present to you the findings that led me to my position, which is: we should not touch, culture or otherwise interfere with this material. It's highly dangerous."

The projection changed to show a long thread of tissue at a high magnification. Taken with a scanning microscope, Tina was well familiar with these images. She used to make them all the time, studying rocks and fragments of ice and other material captured near the rift.

"These cellular blobs are typical of the type of structures we first observed," she said in the recording. It was strange to hear her voice from fifteen years ago.

"The word *organism* isn't one I like to use for this thread of material. In its basic form, it is nothing but a blob of material that contains the four basic elements and building blocks of life. The blobs can be soft, pre-protein based or hard, mineral based. There is no structure in these threads or blobs other than the basic molecular structures. They are literally what scientists used to call the soup of life. But when you grow this material in the lab, it's likely to change in nature overnight, becoming fungus-like or slime-like and resembling known structures.

"If we insert biological material of known origin, say, a lettuce leaf, the alien molecules imitate the cell structures, but at the same time turn the ensemble of leaf plus alien molecules into something different: a live creature of its own. A living lettuce leaf.

"This alien material is more than the building blocks of life. It's able to turn into any kind of life it wants. It's an origin of life. If you're religious, you may call it God's putty.

"We don't know what drives it and what triggers change. Until we know this, the risk of infection through this material is huge. If we come into contact with it, we're likely to become infected. If we're infected, it has the potential to change us and who—or what—we are."

Mentally, Tina filled in what she had wanted to say back then: she believed there was a chance that many people were already infected. She had taken a lot of flak for going everywhere in her protective gear.

"I don't believe that the agency is taking enough steps to prevent the spread and contamination. I have raised this with my superiors, but they haven't addressed my concerns. I believe the agency hires experts to give them advice. I'm an expert. I am of the opinion that this material is highly dangerous. I will no longer be involved in the spread of it, or in the cover-up that hides the danger from the rest of humanity."

She wondered why Vasily had sent all this, and where he was now.

But then she noticed another folder.

CHAPTER TWENTY-FOUR

IN THE EXTRA FOLDER, Tina found a personal message from Vasily to her.

Dear Tina,

By the time you read this I will probably be dead. I don't have much time to record this, because the pirate fleet is following us and the Federacy forces are refusing to help. It's a long story, and I hope you'll hear it one day. I have time to tell you one story today, and that story isn't it.

I've included the recording of your talk in case you can use it to prove that you were concerned about the rift at an early stage. It proves that you are one of the few people who saw this coming and were prepared to speak up about it.

Because there is another side to the story, as I discovered.

It starts a number of years before you joined.

Some people were aware of the material you so aptly called God's putty and its unlimited regenerative potential. They applied to the Federacy to develop this material commercially. Their applications were full of positive opportunities. Imagine, they said, if you can grow human organs to replace diseased ones.

But time and time again, they became frustrated because their applications were refused. I've personally never seen the communication, but I was led to believe the reasons for refusal were related to safety. Around the time you joined, a number of these people left—necessitating your appointment. Those who left took some of their research, against Federacy policies. They contacted private enterprises. They contacted ex-colleagues, offering huge amounts of cash.

There was a transfer of material from the project to people outside the Federacy, now understood to have Freeranger or at least commercial interests.

We traced the possible traitor back to a group of six of our people who attended a scientific meeting on Pandana. Dexter was one of those people. Others were Leon Ming, Bilal Hassad and Jake Monterra who started their own scientific supply company. All of them attended this scientific meeting at Pandana. We believe they passed the material onto someone who either paid them so that they could afford to start the company, or who promised to conduct further research that the agency was not going to perform.

They were paid very well. Nothing more was said.

Then things started to go wrong, with people,

including you and me, questioning the continuous health issues at the research station. You repeated the earlier research without knowing, and got similar results. You raised the alarm. They ignored you.

Why did they ignore you? Because there is still a huge financial interest tied up with the deal they allowed the commercial companies to sign.

Even if all the reports we wrote all point in a worrying direction, they pretended it didn't happen, because several of the top brass in the research division are making corrupt money out of this, and they're afraid to have their cover blown.

Meanwhile, thousands of people have become ill, but because they are pirates, no one cares.

This is what we know about the spread of the condition: most of the time, it's not infectious. The time at which the condition spreads is a process researchers have described as "bloom", a period of intense growth, in which the ends of frond-like growths secrete a pink fluid, which may or may not froth up when it comes into contact with air. The fluid is highly infectious and will quickly establish new growths. We have heard unconfirmed reports that pirates may have handed it out to their prisoners of rival gangs as soap.

All these individuals have become ill.

Not only is their life span much reduced, but they are less human, as they seem to lose the ability to react in a predictable way. They're aggressive. They regress to living like animals, with their aim only to conquer, win and propagate themselves, at all costs.

Sometimes, they're people with growths all over

their skin, but more often, the damage is internal: people living with growths that have fused with their organs, including their brain. Many have died, including about a third of the people who formerly worked at Project Charon. The rest are suspect, or infected, including myself. The infection is slow-acting, so the pirates will kill me before the infection does.

Both the pirates and the Federacy Force are after me.

For the Force, it's very handy to declare the pirates enemies without letting anyone know why they came to be this way, and without telling humanity what to do about it. They think they can contain the problem by annihilating the pirates. They don't want to face disciplinary action from their own high command and face a scandal of epic proportions if it comes out that this crisis is of their own making. They want to avoid the questions that need to be asked: why were people allowed to pass untested material to third parties? How did it come into the hands of the pirates? How much did the upper command know? How much did people in the Assembly know?

We don't know that any alien entity is in control of them, but the condition has joined a large number of formerly separate pirate groups into a large army that is aggressive and expansionist.

They're not only engaged in direct warfare, but they will try to win your sympathy, using people who are visually unaffected.

Whatever you do, don't lend them any assistance. Whatever good intentions they try to sell to you, don't believe them. Whatever deals or money they offer, don't accept them. They will have infiltrated the mainstream authorities. They will offer you opportunities. But if you come back a few months later, they will be ill and barely human. They will kill you. They will torture you. They will destroy us.

A DEEP CHILL went through her.

Holy shit, holy shit, holy shit.

And this message had lain here for years while the menace spread and had come to this area. Everything made sense.

Simon Fosnet and the other men who had come that night, attacking her home. Aggression without cause.

Whatever deals they offer...

And she was here to get the man money—for medical reasons, he said.

Then Jake's offer, to work for him. He "couldn't say" what the project entailed except she'd be working with that same illegally sold biological material.

No, surely he couldn't say anything.

Jake was in this with Dexter. And Dexter was in it for money or power. Dexter only thought about himself. Dexter might even try to get back at her. Was Dexter affected, too?

Why was she selling this ship to fund some sort of pirate venture? She should go and rescue the shop in case the pirates had taken possession of that.

Wait—Did that mean she should keep the ship? She couldn't even think straight.

She needed to go back to Rex. She sent him a message. He didn't reply.

Well, that wasn't helpful.

Tina turned both devices off, put them in her pocket and looked around for something to use as weapon. A hammer from the toolkit would have to do.

Then she stuck her head out the door of the ship. Rasa sat on her blanket in the access tube.

"Have you seen anyone come past?" Tina asked her.

"No."

"Are you sure?"

"I'm sure. Why should I make that up?"

Tina entered the access tube. The geese came waddling forward, ready to go inside. She quickly slid the door shut.

"They think it's their home," Rasa said.

"It's not. I've just managed to clean off all the bird poop."

Tina glanced down the passage in both directions. It was empty.

Holding the hammer under her jacket, she went down the hallway. When she came around the corner, a man was coming the other way. He didn't look suspicious, but she didn't want to risk it, so she turned right, where she found a hall with a lift that stood open.

She entered it.

This lift, of course, took her to the short-term docks, where ships brought supplies for the station. Even if the station offices closed for part of the day, there was still a lot of activity here. Ships were being unloaded, and people were carrying items and wheeling trolleys into storage compartments.

Not all of the deliveries came from large commercial ships. Some of the ships were small merchant vessels. The trade in goods went on day and night. One of the ships even came from Cayelle. It was not a large ship, it had only just arrived, and two burly men in grey station overalls were unloading the cargo.

An older man, presumably the owner of the ship, was telling them to be careful, following them around.

One of the burly men snapped at him in passing. "Let us do our job. We've unloaded many vessels and wouldn't be doing this job if we didn't do it properly. We know what we're doing. Leave us alone."

As the man was saying this, his colleague wheeled a trolley around him and the owner, who stepped back at that moment, ran backwards into the trolley. One of the boxes fell off.

The owner gave a strangled cry. "Now look what you've done."

The man who had dropped the box simply put it back on top of the stack and continued walking.

The owner followed him. "I demand to see your manager. I demand to lodge a complaint."

"Get out of our way, man. Let us do our job, or there will be more accidents."

The owner whirled around and stormed off.

The two men went back into the cargo hold.

Tina noticed that something small had fallen out of the box that had dropped to the floor. Neither of the two men had seen it.

It looked like a bit of fluff, but when she came closer, it turned out to be a spiky cactus seed.

Tina picked it up.

What was this doing here?

They exported cactuses in those boxes? Whatever for?

Vasily's words came back to her. *Whatever deals they offer...*

The shop owner had offered to give her the shop in return for her cactuses. They were special to her because she had done breeding work with them where she had worked out the complicated structure that allowed different species to breed with each other. She had even written a paper about it—holy crap.

Of course, the pirates were after the cactuses, and her specimens in particular, or her knowledge about them. They were alien life. *Semi-sentient* alien life, like she had created by infecting lettuce leaves with the alien matter from the rift.

What if the rift had opened before and material had rained onto Cayelle? The unusual cactuses only occupied a small area of the planet. The plant life in most of the inhabited areas was very different.

The ship had to have come from Gandama.

Hang on—what if they stole her cactuses?

Tina checked the flights from Cayelle and found a couple of ships that fit the merchant's ship's description. All stated Peris City as origin.

One was said to carry agricultural produce, but it was docked on the other side of the central hall. A second ship belonged to a larger commercial company which had its own docking space, but a third was both big enough and in the right area, *and* belonged to a private person, but she did a double-take when she saw the owner's name: J. Monterra.

Yes, it was clear to her now.

Jake had asked her to come and work for him in a "special project" that he couldn't reveal, while he owned a ship that smuggled cactuses from Cayelle, probably knew she was interested in them, and—had he sent Simon Fosnet, or was this a separate incident? On the other hand, how many people could be interested in cactuses?

Not only that, but she realised why Jake wanted her: because she had spent a long time working with the semi-sentient creatures that lived on some worlds. But what was the secret? To interbreed cactuses with other organisms? Animals? People?

Tina stuck the seed in her pocket.

She walked through the old part of the port and then the newer part with the big hall, where a giant screen displayed all the main docks and ships that were arriving or departing. One of the latter was the SS *Stavanger*. That meant Finn's shore leave would have been cancelled.

She went into their hotel and expected Rex to be watching some stupid thing, but the room was empty.

Well, shit.

CHAPTER TWENTY-FIVE

CALM DOWN, calm down.

Likely he'd just gone for a walk. There were plenty of people in the commercial sector and it wasn't as if anyone would do something to him in a busy area.

—Except that pawnshop with the gun. They might sell him illegal stuff he didn't even have money to pay for.

—Except those people who had been following her. They would know him and might try to kidnap him to get to her.

—Except Jake Monterra and his secret project. Or people from the Federacy wanting something from her.

Calm down, calm down.

She sent him another message. Likely, he had just missed the first one.

She waited. She stared at the screen, hoping for a reply that didn't come.

She felt faint with worry. She had to go and look for him.

In the hallway outside the room, the questions ran through her mind. What had happened to him? Why hadn't she insisted that he tell her if he went out? Maybe he had been in trouble and now it was too late.

In her mind, she saw Rex lying in a dingy corridor, a worm without his harness, dying a certain death if she wasn't there to help him.

Somehow she made her way down the stairs and through the reception area.

It was busy in the commercial thoroughfare, and the hand of panic that clamped around her heart made her alternately hot and cold.

There were too many people. She couldn't see anything. She imagined figures lurking in every doorway, behind every dark window, inside every shop. People watched her, gazes following her down the passage. How many of those were spies and how many were just casual observers?

Where was Rex? Where could she ask about him? Which office could she go to and trust?

She searched the moving crowd, the shoppers, the shop assistants, the delivery people.

Rex was nowhere to be seen.

Where could he be and what should she do?

And then she saw him. He was standing with Finn in front of a well-lit shop, deep in discussion.

Well... what was all that about? They didn't look unhappy.

Tina strode to them, making an effort to keep her emotions in check and not to appear agitated.

"There you are," she said.

Rex turned around and looked at her, and she knew she had failed.

"What's wrong with you?" he said.

"Didn't you look at your messages?"

"My…"

He reached for his belt, pulled off the communication device he carried there, and looked at the screen. His face cleared up.

"Oh. I didn't hear it."

"Next time pay more attention. I've just spent half an hour worrying about you."

His face fell. "I'm sorry. I just didn't hear it."

"I thought you were going to stay in our room."

"It was boring, and I decided to go for a walk. You said I could."

That was right; she had. And now she was annoyed with herself for letting her emotions get away with her. Yes, it seemed a lot of people were curious about her, but it was ridiculous to think anyone would try to kidnap Rex to get to her. Especially in a space station, where every step was recorded and the chance of getting caught for committed crimes was very high.

She breathed out tension. "So what have you been doing?"

"I was just looking around here, and then I met Finn."

They both turned to the shop. Finn had moved away from the mother-and-son moment and was standing closer to the window.

A couple of shops had been joined together, and glass installed all down the front. Inside the open and well-lit space people were using exercise equipment, but there was also equipment for sale.

Part of the window advertising space was taken up by various items of body enhancements for sale. An eyepiece proclaimed that the wearer could see close up and in the distance and in different wavelengths and allowed the projection of data figures in the wearer's vision. Leg extensions let you run faster; others attached weights for places where the gravity was low, and still others had magnetic soles for walking on walls in zero gravity.

Against the back of this display area stood a magnificent exoskeleton. It was taller than the one Rex wore now, painted in black and red. The arms were sleek, made out of metal with shining joints. The legs had powerful compressed air pistons that would bounce with every step. Tina recognised them because she had read about these harnesses. The helmet was optional, a cheerful sign said. It displayed a price tag of a cool 5000 credits, and, the cheerful sign continued, it could be adapted to measure overnight at no extra charge.

Indeed.

Rex looked at it in complete silence. Only his eyes moved, from the broad shoulders to the feet that looked just like boots and back again.

It was a beautiful thing.

Yes, she wished she could afford something like that for him. If he wore a harness like that, people on Cayelle would come to him to do their tasks. They would look up to him, they would want him to help them. He would have no trouble finding work, paying work, too. His peers would look at him in amazement, rather than tease him.

But at night he would still need his old mother to change his pants and empty the containers. And his current harness was easy to maintain. She could do it, and if a part broke, it was easy to find a replacement. If this expensive, exquisite exoskeleton broke, she bet that the whole thing would need to be shipped to somewhere far away, from where it would take ages to return. It was just not practical.

She felt almost guilty pulling him away from the shop with the bad news and choices about the future she had to share with him, and she hadn't yet worked out how she would tell it.

"We need to find some dinner."

"It's so beautiful," he said.

"Yes. If you do all your schoolwork, maybe I will think about it."

She didn't know where that came from. The harness she planned to buy for him was much simpler than this one, and she would have to find a hell of a lot of money to be able to afford this thing, let alone pay for its maintenance, but she just couldn't stand the disappointed look on his face.

Rex turned to her. His eyes lit up. "Really?"

"Really." She would do her utmost best.

When they walked away from the shop in the direction of the accommodation, Finn came with them.

This was an unwelcome complication. Maybe Finn had been sent to keep an eye on her. She didn't trust him.

"Don't you have to return to your ship?" Tina asked him. He wasn't even in uniform.

"Not yet."

Tina was going to say something about all personnel having to be on the ship when it was about to leave, but he knew she knew that as well. Something was going on.

"We're going to get some dinner," she said.

"That's all right by me. If I can come."

She wanted to say no, but couldn't bring herself to.

They went back to the accommodation and found an empty table at one of the surrounding eating-houses.

It was not as busy as it had been the previous night, and

Tina gathered that this was because the personnel of the warships had been called in.

She asked Finn, and he told a vague story about the ships departing because they needed to close a route.

"How much do you know about these pirates? Have you ever seen any?"

"Everyone on board the ships gets shown vids. The ones that we've captured are all affected with a skin condition that makes them look like toads. Their methods are arcane. They will try to capture and board a ship rather than shoot it from a distance, and when they do board your ship, you're gone. They fight like madmen, throwing themselves into battle based on the premise that their numbers are limitless."

"Are they limitless?"

"I don't know, but there are certainly a lot of them. Their ships are fast. They're small and can sometimes evade detection."

He changed the subject and asked about the condition she had found her ship in, and suggested things for her to look at before she could sell it.

"I'm a ship's engineer, and I did work some time in a small ship yard," he said. "I know the things that buyers will look at. I can help you."

"So if you're an engineer, why aren't you with your ship now? I have also flown on those big ships, so I know that leave gets cancelled the moment the ship is slated for departure. What are you still doing here?"

He looked down. His mouth worked.

He met her eyes, and there was a guilty look in them. He knew that she knew that his ship had cancelled shore leave.

"You were not on shore leave, were you?"

He breathed out heavily and shook his head. "I had a

disagreement with my superior officer and they decided it was best if I didn't continue my service."

"When did this happen?" He'd still been wearing a uniform last time.

"I was officially released from service this morning."

"Because the ship is leaving."

"Yes."

"Can you talk about what happened?"

"It's a long and very boring story and the details of my life are pretty sordid."

"You're part of the Kaspari dynasty of Olympus?"

He snorted. "You did some digging?"

"A few things didn't add up to me."

"Once a Perseus agent, always a Perseus agent."

"I was a biologist. I didn't do any of the spying stuff. But it was obvious. If you tell me that you're off duty and you're eating alone without any other off-duty troops, I know something is up."

"I guess I'm a bad liar."

Rex was watching with wide eyes. It was good that he saw this, that the Force spat people out when they didn't fit their narrow ideal of what their people should be like.

Finn snorted again and looked at his hands. Just when Tina thought that he wasn't going to say anything else, he started, "Yes, I am that Kaspari." He wasn't looking at Tina or Rex.

"You don't have to talk about it," Tina said.

"I'm out of the Force, so I might as well."

"Only if you want to. I'm not exactly in an easy position either. Neither is my life a paragon of virtue, and I understand if you want to keep certain things quiet."

"I'll soon have to return to my family. They're already

highly unimpressed with my efforts. They'll probably say I'm only suitable to clean their lavatory blocks."

"But you *are* an engineer. I looked it up." Tina briefly considered that he might have bought his way into the Force, but for all that she knew about the recruiting process, and all the bad things that went on inside those ships, hiring people without the appropriate skills was not a thing. When you were out there in space, the lives of thousands of people depended on the engineers. You made sure that they knew what they were doing.

"Yes, I am. Not the kind of engineering that my family appreciates. My family doesn't really appreciate engineering at all. They prefer to leave doing the actual work to the lowly workers. They prefer to do shady deals over lavish lunches."

"I get the feeling that you don't like your family very much."

He laughed. "I thought I was hiding it well."

And then they all laughed.

He shrugged. "Families... You don't choose them. Mine sounds like a highly concentrated news report from the Gossip Channel." He gave a wry chuckle.

"Where do you fit in the family?"

"I'm George Kaspari's black sheep grandson. I'm the one they don't talk about."

"So, can you tell me why you got dismissed?"

"Honourably retired," Finn said.

"Okay, honourably retired." Tina, too, had been honourably retired, because it meant less work for her superiors.

"How familiar are you with engines?"

"Not that familiar. If you're going to talk about engineering, you'll have to do it in lay terms. I'm a biologist."

"Okay. It was my task to do the part of the maintenance that releases fuel into the engine chamber. They wanted me to double the output. I told them that it was likely that would damage the engine, at the very least. At the worst, it would cause significant damage to the ship once the engine reached full capacity."

"Why did they ask you to do this?"

"Because the pirates have extremely fast ships. Much faster than ours. Ours are too big and take too long to reach maximum speed. We have smaller, faster ships, but none are here. The superiors wanted a shortcut to make our ships faster. I told them that things didn't work that way, and things went downhill from there. They accused me of trying to argue with my superior. I explained the argument to them, but in the end they just didn't want to listen. I suspect they'll get one of their lackeys to do it anyway, and probably in another few months time we'll hear about the SS *Stavanger*'s demise. That is if we hear about it at all."

Tina shivered inside. Because that was exactly the way she had been dismissed, for arguing with a superior. Even if that superior was her husband, and if the path that he insisted on was truly suicidal.

But she didn't want to talk about that, so she asked him, "What are you going to do now?"

He shrugged. "Look for a job, I guess."

"You said you worked with small engines?"

"I have."

"Could you check out my ship? I can't pay, but I'll buy your food."

"That's a deal."

"How good are you with weapons?"

"I'm okay. But I need to have a weapon first and I don't."

Tina thought of the magnificent Federacy gun in the display case in the pawnshop. "Other things can be used as weapons."

"Yeah, I guess."

"Rex and I need protection. We would appreciate it very much if you could hang out with us, at least until we've sold the ship. A lot of people have been bothering us, and I'm not sure what's going on."

"What sort of people?"

"Young men mostly, trying to sell us things or services we don't need."

"So you're finding the ship in a less desirable condition than you expected?"

"Not necessarily. If I can get it refuelled, it will work, but it's a bit dusty. We spent most of today cleaning. It's amazing all the black stuff that will grow on the walls when you're not there. We also had a problem with a squatter."

"Oh, they're everywhere. I hope you didn't have too much trouble getting rid of him."

"Her, actually."

His eyebrows flicked up. "What did you do?"

"I told her to be on her way, but she came back, with her geese."

He laughed. "Geese?"

"Yes, seriously. They're quite vicious."

"Well, good on her. If she's got the animals defending her, that's probably why she's still alive."

"She said something about being afraid of gangs, and so I let her stay in the access tube. I presume she'll keep people away from the ship. She's the same age as Rex. I guess I'm just a big softie and I felt sorry for her. I should have reported her to the authorities."

"Heavens, no. The stations can't afford to keep prisoners. Most of these girls get sold off as sex slaves and are never heard from again."

"By the authorities?"

"Oh, they wrap it up in different words. They call it employment, but that's essentially what happens."

They finished their meal. Finn insisted on paying, and went to his accommodation. Tina watched him go.

"What are you doing, mum?" Rex asked. "Do you want him to come and work for us in the shop?"

"Would you like that?"

"Yeah. He's fun. He can be my uncle or brother or something."

Except Tina wasn't sure there would be a shop to return to.

CHAPTER TWENTY-SIX

AFTER FINN LEFT, Tina and Rex went up to their room. Tina wasn't sure how to tell Rex about the things she had learned and the suspicions growing in her mind.

For the first part, down the hallway, they walked in uneasy silence.

Then Rex said, "You said you went back to the ship?"

"Yeah. I forgot something."

"Oh. And the girl had come back?"

"She had. She said she was afraid of the gangs in the other parts of the station."

They reached the door to their room, and Tina opened it, letting them into the slightly musty smell of well-used accommodation.

Then Rex said, "Did you get your thing?"

"I did."

"Where is it?"

Tina showed him the device.

"Whoa! Do they still use those? I thought the Federacy Force used the most modern stuff."

"They do, but this has sat in a locker for fifteen years."

"You're kidding. It's the same one you put in?"

"It is."

"They weren't interested?

"Honestly, I don't know what's going on."

Tina let out a deep sigh. "I don't know that it was such a good idea to come here."

"Why not? Didn't you want to sell the ship?"

"Yes." She *did*. Now she wasn't sure that was such a good idea, either. If it was no longer safe to return to the shop—and how could it be, when the lender would know where she was and would keep coming back for his money, which was his right to ask?

"But?" And Rex was far too smart to be happy with simple answers.

Tina sighed and sat on the bed. "For one, there's your father. You know I don't like talking in a bad way about him."

"You say that all the time and then you follow it up with half an hour of ranting about how selfish he is. Look, I'm used to it. Just tell me he's an arsehole."

Tina cringed. He was probably right. After what he had done, it was impossible for her to talk about Dexter without letting her opinion of him shine through.

She blew out a breath. "I met someone who told me that after the project we worked on was closed, he started a company that may have connections to the pirates."

"What's up with these pirates, anyway? Are they the same ones we had in Cayelle?"

Tina said that they were, and went on to explain in a few sentences what she had learned or surmised: that the pirates had obtained alien material that imitated and infected living tissue, and that they had been allowed to spread this material for years.

"Was that because they didn't read your message?" Rex asked.

"Well, I don't want to give myself that much credit, but things might have been less bad if they had read it."

This raised the question: did an impartial body in the Federacy Force prepared to listen to her story still exist?

She told Rex that some people in Gandama—whom she had personally seen—were infected with the alien material, and that this would gradually turn them into something less than human. And for some reason, they wanted her cactuses.

"But why?" Rex asked.

"I don't know. I think it came about because I wrote a paper about them, but I have no idea how they plan to use them."

"By making a cactus army that zaps you with spikes if you come too close?"

Tina gave a wry chuckle. She wished it was funny, but in reality, everything was possible. Even a cactus army.

"So isn't the answer simple, then? You shouldn't give them the cactuses. Tell Janusz not to let anyone take them."

"I let them loose in the desert."

"Then no one will know where they are."

"I don't know. I did it because they would be safer, not because I thought they would be protected against any kind of theft."

Rex frowned at her, and then she realised he didn't even know that the owner had offered to exchange them for the shop.

His eyes widened when she told him. "But why?"

Tina blew out a breath. From his perspective, it would have been so easy.

"There must be something in the cactuses that is worth a lot. At first I thought he might want to sell them to collectors."

"That could still be true. Some collectors are really crazy."

That was true and they had even seen that since coming here.

"Why didn't you give them to him? It would have solved our problems."

"I didn't think so, and I still don't think so. He wouldn't sign any kind of document that proved ownership of the shop if I gave him the cactuses. I didn't trust him. It was more because of that, than that I didn't want him to have the cactuses. We need the income from the cactuses to survive, but if I'd believed giving them to him would get him off my back, I would have."

"But you mentioned my father. I still don't get what my father has to do with this."

"I'm not sure if he has anything to do with the cactuses in particular, but he was involved with a meeting between people from Project Charon and a commercial interest. At that meeting, an exchange of material took place. It's believed that this material then made it to the pirate fleet, because the pharmaceutical company experimenting with it recruited people allied to the pirates to be their test cases. Your father was involved with a betrayal of the agency and the Force."

"Betray the Force? Why would he do that?"

"Your father only ever wanted two things: money or power, preferably both. And he was impatient and didn't like rules, even if those rules were sometimes very sensible. Maybe he didn't know that the person he sold the samples to was allied with the pirates. It's quite possible. But he definitely knew that he wasn't supposed to sell the material."

"Do you know where he is?"

"No. Maybe he's stuck at Pandana. Maybe with the pirates."

"Would he have turned into one of those..." He made a wriggling movement with his pincers to indicate the warts.

"Maybe. I don't know." The thought made Tina uncomfortable.

Rex asked the next question that Tina didn't want to hear. "What about Evelle? Is she with the pirates, too?"

"I don't think your father and your sister are in the same place anymore. And they haven't been for a long time."

"She's thirty, isn't she?

"Yes, she is, and should be old enough to hold her own rank in the Force."

Then Rex said, "I wonder what my sister looks like."

"You can find pictures of her in the Force's systems."

Tina had looked at them, barely recognising the pixie-like creature with the short spiked-up hair.

"What if they were both in trouble?"

"They could be, but in that case I don't see what we could do. I can't live with what-ifs. If they contact us, I'd have to think about what to do. It's not like your father has ever been nice to me or you. We don't owe him anything."

"What if there was no one else?"

"Well..." Tina took in a deep breath. What if people who were infected had made a threat to Dexter or had offered him something he wanted? More money and freedom to do research would sway him to at least attend a meeting. Yes, he was greedy, but he would spend that money on research, not on himself. For all the bad things she could say about Dexter, he wasn't the sort of person who wasted a lot of money on frivolous things.

It wasn't that much of a stretch to think that he'd been swayed by promises for funds and facilities, that turned out to be too good to be true, and he'd realised too late. Possible that he'd been dumb rather than malicious.

She had almost been taken for a ride by the lender and his "medical" condition. He'd wanted the cactuses. Anyone except her would have just given him the collection to retain her business.

But people had betrayed her before, so she was cautious.

And another thought: how long had this been going on?

Her marriage to Dexter had never been particularly close, but it worked until he began to push his work in directions that she thought were questionable. At one stage, he even wanted to use an agency ship to send people into the rift. That was just stupid. She told him so, and he got angry. It wasn't just a disagreement, but a fight that had scared her.

He told her not to be ridiculous. Then he accused everyone of being too timid, and said sometimes you needed to make sacrifices in order to move forward. They'd been hanging around this rift for over thirty years. Wasn't it time that something was done?

Heavens, what if he had already been infected at the time? And if so, what did that mean for Rex?

She helped Rex get ready for bed, washing him and giving him his injection and making sure that the attachment points were all clean.

She had always assumed that his condition was due to the fact that she had spent too much time in space while pregnant, but what if his deformities came from having been born of a man infected with alien material? It was just too horrible to think about.

She couldn't help feeling inadequate because he had to walk around in this harness that people wanted him to sell to collectors. And she had far too many other things to worry about. Rex always came somewhere down the list of priorities.

There was a knock on the door.

She frowned at Rex, in his pyjama bag, ready for bed. "Did you order something?"

"From that expensive room service? Of course not."

The knock came again.

Tina went to the door and found one of the receptionists in the hallway.

"Someone wants to speak to you," he said.

"Someone?" Tina frowned. She didn't know anyone. Other than Dexter, who clearly did not want to speak to her. Other than Jake, and she didn't want to speak to him, either.

"Look, tell him I'm—"

"It's someone from the planet below."

That was even stranger. But she went with the receptionist, and he took her to a small and cluttered communication cubicle behind the reception area.

She was well familiar with these sorts of things, and had often seen people use them, especially when she was out in space and they visited the stations. It wasn't allowed for personnel to contact their families from the ship, because the ship's location was secret.

Inside the small cubicle, the operator told her how to use the equipment.

When she touched accept, an image came on the screen before her.

Out of all the possible people it could have been, the image showed Janusz. She could barely believe her eyes. Why in the world would he contact her? "Hello."

"I bet you're wondering what I've got to say," he said.

"I would be lying if I said I wasn't."

"It's not good news, I'm afraid. But I wanted to tell you, just so that you understand that I have nothing to do with this, because I am sure to get the blame if you find out from anyone else."

Tina's heart was thudding. Something had obviously happened.

"It was two days after you left," Janusz started. "I woke up one night and heard a racket next door, so I grabbed the gun and went out to check. Someone had broken into the shop again by cutting through the roller door. When they heard me, they ran out, throwing a firebomb over their shoulder. So I was caught between putting out the fire and chasing the miscreants. I chose the fire because I figured you'd want your shop when you come back."

"Thank you." Although she had no warm and fuzzy notions about why he had done it: he'd wanted to limit risk to his own property.

"So the miscreants disappeared into the desert, and no one has seen them since. I managed to put out the fire, but I'm afraid there's some damage to the back of the shop."

"Have you reported this to the authorities?"

"That, I have. People can't go around burning shops, much as we like to do our own thing in Dickson's Creek."

"What did they say?"

"They came out here and walked around for a whole day,

collecting things and taking pictures. They said there had been earlier trouble."

"That was probably about the earlier attack on my shop. Did the thieves take anything?"

"That's the strange thing. It looks like they left the stock untouched, but rummaged through all the records on the shelves next to the desk and the drawers on the counter. All that stuff was on the floor. Never knew how much all those trinkets are worth to be honest."

Tina cringed. He'd been looking at her books and stock purchases. "Any idea why they didn't touch the stock?"

"Nah. Looking for money's my guess. I don't know what was there, and I don't know what you took and what you left here and what you put in storage. I didn't even know where you were gone, to be honest, which was why I didn't report it for so long. I thought there would be trouble, and I thought you were dead."

Well, thanks so much for that. "Has anyone from the city been there to visit?"

"There've been plenty of folk, but I'm not going out there to talk to them or ask their names, because I don't want to be involved. All I want to say was that I had nothing to do with the break-in and fire, I want you to understand that."

"Well thanks for keeping an eye out," Tina said.

"Any word on when you'll be back?"

Tina was going to tell him that she would be back as soon as possible, but she had second thoughts about that. She had never trusted him, and she wasn't about to start, although she did believe that he didn't have anything to do with this fire. If he'd wanted to terrorise her out of Dickson's Creek, he'd had fifteen years to do it. He wouldn't have needed to wait until she was gone.

"I am not sure when I'll be back yet," Tina said. "Could be a few days."

After she had signed off and was on her way back to her room, a realisation hit her. There was no way in which he could have figured out where she was, unless someone had told him.

That meant they were watching her, whoever "they" were. Simon Fosnet. The thieves. Jake Monterra.

People who wanted to drive her into cooperating with them.

They weren't interested in her stock or money—of which there wasn't terribly much anyway—but they wanted her records. Her cactuses that she had bred and written a research paper on. They wanted her data.

But what was so special about these cactuses?

The research paper that hadn't yet come out contained a summary of her knowledge. The cactuses were limited to a small area of the planet, the desert outside Gandama. They seemed to have developed coping strategies against attacks by local wildlife, mainly armadillos. They exhibited properties normally reserved for introduced species. They were unaffected by local pests and diseases.

She had a lot more data generated by her work. Experiments that hadn't yet led anywhere worth reporting on. Projects that weren't yet completed. Hey, she was doing this for *fun*, and nobody told her what she needed to cover in her research.

No matter how often they turned over the shop in Gandama, thieves and spies wouldn't find this data. She had brought it with her.

She couldn't believe Rex's joke that the pirates were

breeding a prickly army, but obviously they wanted the cactuses for some reason.

It was also clear that if she went back to the shop, pretending to do business as usual, these people would continue to put pressure on her, and her safety would be compromised.

Not just her safety, but Rex's. And he didn't deserve this.

Besides, she had already done that once, when she resigned from the Force and disappeared from public life, and see where that had led. No, she couldn't live with herself if she did that. She would forever look at Rex and know that his life was going to be in danger if she did nothing.

She would stop these criminals or die trying. She had spent too much time already assuming that Dexter and Evelle were safely getting on with their lives. It was time to start doing something.

So...

She had a ship, and information the pirates wanted. What else could she do with it other than going to Olympus and presenting it to the Federacy Assembly?

If they were still honourable enough to do the right thing. And she had to hope for that, because otherwise what was the point of anything?

Well, crap. That changed her plans somewhat.

CHAPTER TWENTY-SEVEN

TINA SNEAKED BACK into the room. The light in the corner was still on, but Rex had fallen asleep in her absence, so she grabbed her notepad and left the room again.

In the bar behind the reception desk, she ordered a drink before finding herself a spot in the corner.

When the going got tough, the tough... made a budget.

While sitting at the table waiting for her drink to turn up, she made a table of all the necessary expenses. Some she could avoid. She felt happy to hoodwink the local authorities, but she would not defraud businesses. Deferring payments might be a necessary evil.

She had six thousand in savings. How much was it going to cost to get to Olympus?

She might be able to get ninety thousand for the ship.

If she sold it, she had the money to buy tickets, or she could use the ship to get around independently. Selling it would take too much time, but keeping the ship left her with the issue that she wouldn't have any money to buy the things she needed to get it out of dock. Important stuff like fuel, provisions and the remaining fees for the ship to be released from the station. Maybe even a pilot to navigate the ship out of the tight position where it had become stuck.

That was presuming she didn't find any technical issues that needed to be fixed first.

She didn't know how much those things would cost, except for the station fees, and they were two and a half thousand. But maybe she could use Louise Metvier to get the fees waived.

Or, if worse came to worst, she could get Rex to disconnect the ship from the station without paying. That backdoor into the dockside computer system he had discovered might be handy.

How much was a refuel worth these days?

She looked it up: twelve hundred. But there was an eight hundred extra charge for "fast service" to cut fuelling time from two days to half an hour.

What about food supplies for the journey to Olympus? Likely to be two thousand.

What about docking fees at Olympus? Another two thousand.

What about her outstanding bill for accommodation? Fifteen hundred.

The air recyclers needed to be recharged, too, and she couldn't leave without the latest updates in navigation, and meanwhile Benny had been running up a bill while updating himself.

Crap, she already needed more than she had.

She could probably wrangle five thousand in credit.

And she hadn't even thought about the need to have crew on board. She remembered all too well how stressful it had been to fly the ship alone, and that was without a son who needed her for his daily functioning.

Come to think of it, how was Rex going to sleep in the ship when he couldn't access any of the cabins? Or get into the luggage compartment to get tools or other items if she needed them?

Finn. He was from Olympus. He might not be too keen on a ride home, but in her experience, certain types of well-off people rarely turned down an offer for a free ride. Because if they liked spending money, they wouldn't be well-off.

He seemed OK, apart from the fact that his family owned a pharmaceutical company which may or may not have been involved in receiving illegal material from Dexter. But even if that was so, she didn't think Finn had anything to do with it. And an engineer would be an asset to have on board.

Finn was coming, even if he didn't know it yet.

But taking in an extra person would mean a bigger food supply, and an increased cost. It was time to get creative.

She would ask the ship suppliers to deliver a resupply and refuel package to the ship on credit. The five thousand would probably cover the accommodation bill as well. It would rack up big amounts in interest while she wasn't paying it off, but that was a problem for later.

Fuel. She needed some ingenuity for that. A fast refuel would take only half an hour. She'd have to make up some excuse why it was necessary to charge the ship.

That left two vitally important items. The first one would be relatively easy, but required some preparation. The second, she would have to pay for.

Both needed to be done tonight.

She found an online listing of Federacy Force insignia,

found a special agent badge and pasted the name L. Metvier over it. The 3D printing shop worked around the clock, and rather than risking her order being flagged, she went to the shop with her model on a data stick.

It was for a party, she explained to the attendant who delivered her the fake badge.

The thing was a bit crude, but since few people knew what these badges really looked like, it would have to do. She worked the uneven edges away with a screwdriver, stuck it in her pocket, and walked through the near-deserted commercial passage.

The gym was still closed, although a light was on in the depth of the shop. The pawn shop, however, was open. The gun still lay in its case, an illegal weapon that belonged to the Federacy Forces.

She went straight through the door and up to the counter.

The shop owner lifted his eyebrows. He knew this was going to be trouble.

"How can I help you?" he said. "Have you got something to sell, something you want to buy?"

Tina pulled out her fake badge. She doubted the man could read, but she bet he knew how to recognise the symbols of the Federacy.

"I'm agent Metvier, from the Perseus Agency. I am here to lay claim on that weapon you have in the case over there."

The man looked from the badge to her, his eyes widening. He opened his mouth several times and shut it again.

Finally he said, "I thought there was something fishy about it."

"Then why didn't you give it over to any of the soldiers who were just at the station?"

His mouth opened further. He stammered, "I—I didn't think they had time."

To be fair, the troops had been on leave, and would probably not have been interested, seeing that they probably found contraband material everywhere they went.

"I'm here now, and that is an illegal weapon."

"Yes, yes, sure."

He reached under the desk, and pulled out a little device which he took over to the cabinet, and opened the back of it. He took out the weapon and brought it to the counter, where he laid it in front of Tina.

"Here you go." There was sweat on his forehead and he seemed very nervous all of a sudden.

With an equally trembling hand, Tina picked up the weapon, and coolly inserted it into a plain bag.

"I hope this means there won't be any charges?" the man said.

"I will look into that. You've been very cooperative." And Tina walked out the shop.

She mentally crossed one expense off the list. Weapon. Tick.

But now she had to hurry because his story would hit the gossip circuits pretty soon.

Once she was a safe distance from the shop, she pulled out the weapon to familiarise herself with the make and type. The Fireseed312 was not significantly different from her old 301.

She wondered how it had fetched up here, but she doubted she would ever know. For now, her disguise as a Federacy agent was as complete as it was going to get. Her fake identity would probably start to circulate soon, so time was of the essence. It was time for the next step.

She went to a ship supply business and was happy to see that they did air, food and water supply of ships. She tacked on an order for Rex's medicine. And a fast refuel.

Her ship hadn't been cleared for departure but, business being business, there was only a single question about that, which Tina quickly dismissed with, "That will all be fixed by mid-morning. I've got an urgent job."

They took her credit and said they'd deliver the food parcels within an hour. They'd start the refuel job once the ship was at the top of the queue, which would be another fifteen minutes.

Done.

Now the next thing.

CHAPTER TWENTY-EIGHT

THEN IT WAS on to the hard part: obtaining permission to leave the station. Without the necessary payment or resolution about outstanding fees, that was going to be hard. But Tina had proof of what she'd already paid, and hoped that her Federacy ID might do the job if she spoke convincingly about a secret project.

It was still reasonably busy in the Port Authority office, but obtaining a ticket for *private craft departures* allowed her to bypass most of the queues.

The woman at the counter asked her some basic questions about her destination—Tina mentioned she was going to a nearby station in the system—and crew. Tina said it would be just her and one crew member.

Then she asked about any cargo and wanted to see a thing called a *shipping docket* and Tina said she didn't have any cargo.

But the woman kept saying that she needed a shipping docket. Apparently it was something new, and one had to obtain a formal declaration of the commercial, or non-commercial, status of the items on board the ship.

Eventually she agreed for Tina to see a supervisor. She let Tina into a small office behind the counter and told her to wait there. And then she left, letting the door fall closed with a click. Tina's heart jumped.

Was that...?

She rose and tried the door handle. It was locked.

Well, shit. What now?

So she looked around the room. Apart from the desk, there was another chair, and on the desk was a computer screen, that displayed a picture of the Federacy logo.

That was her best chance.

Years ago, as part of the Perseus Agency staff training, she had done a course in the most basic tricks for getting into systems or out of locked doors by using the security system against itself. She had refined that knowledge with years of experience in best practices in smaller security systems, and knew the flaws.

She bet that when she left fifteen years ago, they had erased all her data from the system. She knew this could sometimes take a long time and a lot of reminding. Since she hadn't been there to remind them, the data was very likely to still be on the system. One would think that military operations were more diligent than to leave old personnel files, but with the closing of Project Charon, no one would have thought to close their access portals, letting them just fade into obscurity.

She went up to the screen and gave it her best secret agent stare. The Federacy logo disappeared. The screen unlocked.

Seriously, how dumb was that? They might have erased

her name from the employee list, but they left her retina scan on the system.

The screen displayed the program where the woman had been entering information about Tina and her ship. All of Tina's information was still displayed on the screen, including what she had told the woman today.

In the assessment window down at the very bottom, it said, *Possibly dangerous. May be enticed to work against the Federacy and in particular the Perseus Agency. Has detailed knowledge about the working of Project Charon. Should be handled with care. Contact Jake Monterra.*

Sure enough. This was Jake's doing.

No way would she talk to Jake. She did not want to accept his job offer, or let him anywhere near her research results or her data from the project or her cactuses.

The computer wouldn't let her past the displayed form, insisting that she enter a station employer ID. If this was like all other systems, any attempts at guessing would be blocked after a few tries.

This was going to require a few interesting tactics. She preferred just to break out of the room the old-fashioned way. She went to the door again, and tried with a bit more force to open it. But it was definitely locked.

Then she looked around the room trying to find if she was being monitored. She found a small hole near the ceiling. She took a piece of rag out of her pocket and stuffed it inside. She also hung another rag over the air vent.

She listened at the door.

It was completely quiet in the hallway, with just the faintest sound of voices drifting from the main room.

The door looked much too solid to be bashed down, so she would have to be smart about this. But her pockets did not include anything that she could use to open doors. Maybe she could use something from the room.

There was only the computer, and the furniture. The desk did not have a drawer, and there were no cupboards or shelves in the room.

She did have a pair of pliers, but not the type that would cut anything.

With the pliers she managed to pull the computer's lead out of the wall. But there was no thread inside that she could pull out and use, so she put it back. She would have to unlock the door electronically, but that would leave evidence in the system.

The computer didn't like having been turned off.

It came up with a menu that said *Confirm your identity*.

What? No backup batteries? She again stared at the screen.

Crap.

She tried looking at the screen again, and was told the entry was incorrect. Then she tried her false identity Louise Metvier access code, but it was incorrect, too. She hesitated about whether this was worth revealing her third identity, but her hesitation was brief. Rex was alone and she needed to get back to him and the ship, and then she needed to get the hell out of here. With or without permit.

Then she'd worry about what to do next.

She pulled out her third identity number, and when she tried it, the screen unlocked.

It said, *A possible security breach has been recorded. Do you want to check the room or unlock it.* She remembered this part of station or ship protocol. It did this so that people would never be locked inside their rooms in an emergency.

Tina chose unlock it.

A click sounded inside the door. She tried the handle, and it moved aside.

But now she was faced with the next problem: how to get past the people in the office? Especially since someone there was likely to be armed. And as soon as she revealed her gun, all hell would break loose.

She checked the hallway. It was empty. The sound of voices drifted in from the far side.

She turned left in the direction of the main office. Her hand was in the bag, clutching the handgrip of the gun.

At the door, she hesitated and peeked inside. There were so many people in there. She couldn't see the woman who had shut the door on her, but a number of security people stood at the entrance to the waiting area, waiting for authorities to turn up to arrest her, no doubt.

Tina couldn't see their weapons, but they would be armed. She would have to be quick or bold.

She stepped into the room. A young man turned around, and before he could ask what she was doing there, she said, "I need to check on the Charon files." Total nonsense, of course.

Without waiting for his reaction, she walked through, slipped to the other side of the counter and left the office past the security guards who were chatting with a man.

It was only when she was a bit further down the passage that she heard a shout.

"Hey, ma'am, stop."

Nope. Definitely not.

Tina walked away as quickly as she dared without running. That was still drummed into her. Don't run. Never run, or your guilt will be assumed.

But she ducked into the first side passage. Then she ran.

And turned right, and ran down that passage as well, until she was out of breath. It was a long time ago since she had done any running.

Crap, that was close.

Now she had a few more things to do, and she hoped she could do them before the ticking time bomb exploded.

CHAPTER TWENTY-NINE

BEING AN EX-MILITARY OFFICER, Finn turned out to be much more of a morning person than Rex was. There were no proper days in space and Rex hated getting up when it was still dark.

She met Finn in the foyer of the place where he was staying, much fancier than her own accommodation.

His mouth fell open when she told him about her plan. "You want to—what?"

"I'm offering you free passage to Olympus."

"Yes, but I might as well kill myself now, because this will destroy all opportunity for me to ever work in the Force, or in any official position, again."

"Do you want to? Serving in the Force doesn't tend to suit people with strong ideas."

It was true and he knew it, even if he said nothing in reply.

Tina continued. "Your career in the military is ruined, like mine. It's a reality. They will never re-employ us, because even if we're 'honourably discharged', everyone will know there was nothing honourable about it."

"But I don't want to be considered a danger to the Force."

"We're not."

"Are you kidding? If you pull this stunt, every form of law enforcement is going to be after us."

"The Federacy Force is not law enforcement, and besides, they're too busy with pirates."

He shook his head. "I don't know about that."

"Take it or leave it. I could use an engineer. I'm leaving as soon as I can get a few other jobs done. The only people after me are the station authorities and I have proof that they've been infiltrated by pirates. I'm going to present that evidence to the Federacy Assembly, if anyone out there is still listening."

"Wait, wait. You're saying that this station is run by pirates?"

"People affiliated with pirates at the very least. They're after me and my research. They've tried offering me jobs and money and tried scaring me, breaking into my property. I have the information they want. I'm going to take it to Olympus."

And then she told him about the multiple break-ins to her shop, the letter and strange meeting with Jake Monterra, and the skin condition that spread from the alien material that Dexter and Jake spread to the pirates.

Finn's eyes were wide. "You mean people get grey warty skin and their fingers look short and stubby and their nails grow into claws?"

"Yes. Have you seen people like that?"

"On this station, yes. I assumed it was a local disease

caused by exposure to the weird plant life down on the planet."

"It's not." She also told him about her research from fifteen years back and how Vasily's message had put all the facts together for her.

"So you're saying these pirates are taking over space with an army of monsters?"

"Something like that."

"But if it's just a disease, then they're not all pirates."

"No, but it's a disease that renders people into shells of their former selves. They're likely to be unsuited for duty, after which the pirates only need to come along, promise them something, and they're ripe for the picking."

He nodded slowly.

"And they want my research on cactuses for some reason I don't yet understand."

"Are you sure? They could be after your work for the agency."

"They don't need me for that. They have Jake and Dexter. Those know far more than I do. Vasily, too. Also, I put every-thing I knew in a locker on the station where someone from the Federacy could retrieve it."

He nodded. "I'm familiar with the system."

"And they never looked at it. The package sat in the box untouched for fifteen years."

"Did you tell them about it back then?"

"I did."

"What does that mean for your plan to go to the Assem-bly? Do you think they're going to take any action now?"

Tina shrugged. "Any other ideas for what to do? I'm listening."

"I have some relatives who might be able to help."

"Any that you're not in conflict with?"

Finn sighed. "There is that."

"Any who are not involved in pharmaceutical companies who might have been interested in the alien material and the stuff they call God's putty?"

He gave her a sharp look.

"Don't tell me they *weren't* interested."

His cheeks coloured. "My father was. My uncle said it was dangerous. My father said it could ruin us if we didn't get involved. I think everyone did, ourselves and all our competitors. I don't know that my family ever received anything. I was only a teenager back then and my relationship with my father has never been good."

Did she believe that? "We have to try to set the record straight and uncover anything illegal done by companies or the Force."

"Yes. We do."

They were silent for a while, and then Tina said, "I wonder what happened to Vasily."

He'd said he'd probably be dead in his message. But then again, if he'd been followed and hadn't made it, how would his message have ended up in her document box?

That was a strange mystery.

Finn looked up Vasily Demetrov. "There are no entries about him in the last ten years."

"And before that?"

"Very limited. It says he was employed as ship medic on the SS *Faroe*, but nothing after that."

"What sort of ship is that?"

"It's a communication hub."

That also made sense to Tina. As medic, Vasily wouldn't have been in the know about how these document boxes worked, but on that ship, people would deal with them all the time.

"He seems to have fallen off the records at that time. No word about how or why he left the Force and where he is now."

Unusual, at the very least. "That means he's either still there or he's dead."

"There would be a record of his death," Finn said. "Especially if it happened on the ship."

True. "He might be imprisoned for treason."

She shuddered. Ten years of prison for telling the truth? Surely there was another explanation.

Somewhere in the passage outside the hotel's lobby, a shop owner opened a door with a loud rattle of metal.

Tina checked the time. The ship would be almost in the refuel queue. "I have a few other jobs to do. You know what I'm doing and why. Get ready, take your possessions and meet me in the main hall."

She left him sitting at the table. He said he'd be there, but she also sensed a lot of hesitation. Defying your rich family to sign up for the Force was one thing, but working against them another.

It remained to be seen if he would be there. It was time for the final part of her plan.

CHAPTER THIRTY

TINA CAME BACK to the accommodation early in the morning shift.

Rex was still asleep, and she barged into the room with the words, "Get all your stuff. We're getting out of here."

Rex turned around in bed and mumbled, and Tina went through the usual ritual of getting him ready and putting him in the harness.

He made a show of collecting some of his things, but Tina was much quicker.

"Where are we going?" he asked. He sounded grumpy. He was not a morning person. "What's the hurry? You haven't sold the ship. I don't want to go home yet."

"I'm not selling."

Rex stared at her, a deep frown on his face. "You—what? Don't you need the money for the shop?"

"It's all a ruse. The shop is not safe anymore. I was never meant to return. They want me for their evil operations."

"Hang on. Who is 'they'?"

"Come on, I'll explain later. It's getting hot in here."

"What do you mean? I don't think it's hot at all."

"It's a way of speaking. It means that I want to get out of here as soon as we can. There are things afoot which I don't like at all."

She turned around and he let out a surprise squeak. "Mum, how did you get that gun?"

"I confiscated it in the name of the Federacy."

"From the pawn shop?"

"That's the one."

"You mean you forced that guy to give it up."

"That's pretty much the same thing, isn't it? He was not supposed to have it in the first place."

"You stole it?"

"Confiscated it." Frankly, she was a bit annoyed with this sudden concern for the shop owner. They had much more pressing things to worry about.

"Listen, this is a Federacy gun." She tapped the barrel. "I have no idea what happened to the owner, but the pawn shop has no right to sell it."

"Don't want you to go and find the owner?"

"Not now. Right now, I want to get out. If you have a death wish, you can go and find him. Come on, I've got the ship waiting to be refuelled and made ready."

"You—what?"

"We're leaving. I paid the hotel. When you're done questioning, come with me. There is something that I need you for."

Finally, they were out the door, dragging their bags.

Tina was keen to get out before the hotel owner found that her credit bounced.

Rex was still grumbling about having to get up so early while they walked along the passageway. It was not yet late enough for most of the shops to be open, but the shop managers were arriving and turning on the lights inside.

Rex's eyes opened wide when they came to the exercise and body enhancement shop where the black and red harness was no longer in the window display. "It's gone," he said, his voice sad. He looked around as if he would see someone walking around in that magnificent thing in the passageway.

"Come on," Tina said. She led the way into the shop.

Rex looked sideways at her.

"Come on."

He followed her through the shop in between the exercise equipment where a woman, who ran like crazy, raised her eyebrows at Rex as he came past.

She wouldn't be so dismissive when he came back.

The shop manager showed Tina and Rex and into the studio at the back.

In the middle of the room stood the black and red harness. The shop attendant had undone the joints of the arms, and they lay on the table against the wall.

"Go ahead. It's almost ready for you. Make yourself comfortable. Do you want some tea?"

"Yes, please."

"I'll arrange that. Wait here." He walked to the door.

"Mum," Rex said.

The shop owner left the room and shut the door to the studio.

Rex said again, "Mum, we can't afford this. You said it yourself."

"I know. But I'll tell you about all of it later."

"You're not going to do anything illegal?"

"No. I'll tell you later. Honest."

"But I don't want you to get into trouble."

"Honestly, the last few days I've felt ashamed for letting you walk around in that old thing. I should have done something about it much sooner."

"But you said the parts would be hard to get."

"Not that hard. I was just stupid. I just tried too hard to keep you my little boy, and I didn't want to lose you."

"Who says I would ever leave you?"

"I know you want to. No, don't say anything. You want to and you should step into the world, not hide in some backwater with inferior technology, and I should stop putting obstacles in your way. Being independent means going where you want."

"Mum, I don't want to leave you." His eyes glittered.

"Aren't you lucky that everyone is coming, then?"

"Everyone?"

"You and me and Finn."

His eyes widened. "Really? He's coming?"

The door opened again and the shop owner returned with a young man. "Let my employee take your measurements, and he will adapt it for you."

The shop attendant took Rex to a bench at the back of the room, and Tina sat down to drink her tea.

Then she wandered through the exercise centre.

It wasn't busy. Tina walked past the treadmills and bikes and a row of contraptions with weights. Gym visits were essential to staying healthy in space, and she had detested them. It was a little better if you had a private ship and didn't need to share a cramped room with other smelly people, but Tina hated the gym culture, the types that usually hung around and preened themselves in the mirror.

She spent some time looking at the displays of fit, beautiful people on the walls, and then the cabinet with bottles of supplements for sale.

Some sort of commotion seemed to be going on outside.

A lot of people were walking past in the same direction, and some of them were military people. She hadn't thought any were still on the station after the *Stavanger* left.

She hoped Finn had found his way to the dock hall and hadn't gotten caught up in whatever military operation was going. She'd checked his name and he hadn't been taken off the staff list yet. She knew this could take a couple of days and hoped she was right to trust him.

An announcement was made, but the sound was garbled and she couldn't hear it very well.

She wished the shop owner and Rex would hurry up. She was ready and wanted to get out of here. It would be hard enough without a permit.

Finally the door to the studio opened. Rex stood in the doorway. The only way she knew it was him was because of his face, beaming, at the top of the harness.

It was beautiful, consisting of a number of segments that gleamed in the light.

He walked slowly into the room. There were no big thudding footsteps and creaking of armour. There was no more clattering and rattling. He moved soundlessly. Little blue lights lit up when the joints engaged.

He turned around in the aisle that would previously have been too narrow for him. He looked at himself in the mirror, placing his new hand—which actually looked like a metal hand and not a glorified pincher—on the section that encircled his waist.

"Look, it's even got places for guns."

The shop owner explained to her that the harness had a decent amount still to grow in case Rex grew any bigger.

Tina might be broke, but this expense—and it was the only thing she had honestly paid for today—and the look on his face was worth every bit.

"Mum, you haven't even seen the best thing." He lifted up a flap at the front. "I don't have to wear a pad any more. I can go to normal toilet like a normal person."

Tina knew. This was why she wanted the harness for him now. When they were out in space, she wouldn't have the resources to deal with nappies.

Whatever happened, and however she would maintain his harness when they travelled or were back on Cayelle, Tina would find a way.

The shop owner obviously didn't sell these every day, and was most keen to explain all the different features. It came with a suite of instructions, and with Rex being as inquisitive as he was, Tina had no doubt that he would find out all these things by himself, but he delighted in running on the treadmill and lifting weights with his new arms. He was strong. Somehow she had a feeling that would come in handy, too, one day.

Tina kept looking outside, because something was definitely going on now. They really needed to get moving.

"Do you know what's happening?" she asked when the shop owner gave her an opportunity.

"What do you mean?"

"There seems to be some sort of ruckus out there."

He didn't know.

They needed to get out of there, so she finalised the rest of the transaction as quickly as possible, and left the shop with Rex.

She could almost not hear him walk. It was eerie.

"Are you happy now?" she asked him.

"Mum, where did you get the money for this?" Rex asked. "I didn't think we had enough for this and the hotel and everything else."

"Let me tell you a secret: we don't. But I found out some stuff I'll talk to you about later. We're going to Olympus and we're giving Finn a ride. I've got the ship fuelled, I've bought supplies, and we're leaving right now because if anyone comes to me with another bill, I will not even be able to pretend I'm paying it. We're getting out of here now."

They left the commercial passage and turned to the entrance to the docks. This time, their speed of walking was limited by how fast Tina could walk. Yes, age was catching up with her, and the good life had left her less fit and trim than she used to be.

A lot of military personnel were still rushing past in the same direction. They didn't even give Tina and Rex a second look.

While they walked, Tina picked up talk of an imminent pirate fleet attack in the area from discussions between military personnel.

She tried her comm. *Finn? Are you in the hall?*

He said he wasn't.

Are you at the ship?

I am. Someone else is here. She won't let me through.

That's Rasa. Tell her I sent you.

I did. She doesn't believe me.

Rasa was doing her job too well. *Just get into the ship and start the checks and scans.*

It would be hard enough getting out of the tangled mess of ships and cables once they were loose from the station.

The more slowly they could do this, the better. The refuelling situation had to be taken care of, too. She hoped the ship supplies had been delivered.

A new message came onto the news screens along the walls. *Station alert. Have you seen this person?* It was accompanied by a photo Tina knew well.

"Hey mum, that's you."

It was, too, an old photo from the time of her employment with the agency. This was Jake's doing. "So it is. Let's make ourselves scarce."

"And then you talk about me behaving. What did you *do*?"

"It seems the station's authorities are compromised."

An alarm started blaring in the passage.

Shit. That was probably triggered by facial recognition.

"What does that mean?" Rex asked. "What do you mean, compromised?" His voice sounded high.

"Come on. I believe you can run now. Let's run."

She set off along the passage, and Rex followed her. He was still carrying both their bags, but it took him no effort at all.

Somewhere in the station, a crash made the structure shudder.

"What was that?" Rex squealed.

"Nothing good."

A voice came through the loudspeakers. "All residents please take note. All residents must go to their living quarters or emergency stations. This is not a drill. We're under attack. All residents to emergency stations."

Then a man's voice yelled, "There!"

They had arrived at the docking hall, and the scene was one of mayhem. People were streaming in from all sides, out of other passages, on their way to the lifts, presumably to try to leave the station. People yelled and crowded in front of the lift doors. Mostly doors to the 1 and 2 sectors.

The light of the sector 1 lift flashed, and a moment later, the door opened. A number of strangely clad men burst in, all of them heavily armed and ready for fighting action. They wore pirate belts—proper, well-used ones with weapons, ammunition supplies, knives and pilfered loot dangling from them.

People screamed and pushed away from the lifts. Some dropped to the ground for fear of becoming a target.

A man ran for the railing shooting indiscriminately at the fleeing citizens.

A couple of Federacy Force soldiers came in from the other side and took up the defence. "Come on, quick," Tina said. Her hand itched to get involved, but that would be a dumb move, unless she wanted the Federacy to know she was using an illegal weapon.

"Who are those men?" Rex asked.

"Pirates. I think Jake has called them in." She wondered what the clang was that they'd heard earlier. Surely not even pirates would be dumb enough to compromise the structure of the station?

The lift door opened again, and more invaders streamed into the main hall. They were clad in full body armour and helmets. Tina could almost imagine that they were covered in grey-skinned warts, even if she couldn't see whether or not they were.

They carried weaponry she had never seen. There was no point in trying to shoot back.

Getting out was the only option and many other people

had come to the same conclusion. They all queued in front of the sector 2 lift.

But no one had any interest in the A sector lift, which stood wide open.

Tina and Rex ran along the wall, zigzagging between people, then crossed to the lift. Tina hoped no one saw them go in. The doors closed.

CHAPTER THIRTY-ONE

AS THE LIFT jumped into motion, Tina contacted Finn again. *Are you inside the craft?*

Yes. But I can't get rid of the girl. She's scared.

Damn. They would just have to deal with Rasa. Tina wasn't looking forward to that. *Start the engine warm-up process.*

But we don't have a station pilot yet.

Coming up.

Tina of course hadn't ordered a pilot to take her out of the maze of the docks because she had no permit to leave, but she didn't need to incriminate herself any more than necessary by making her intentions clear.

The lift stopped. The door slid open.

The hall outside was eerily quiet after the noise from the main hall. All Tina could hear was the thudding of her and Rex's footsteps. Hers mainly, because Rex walked quietly.

All kinds of worry went through Tina's mind: whether their food supplies had been brought, and whether Rex and

Benny would be able to detach the ship. If they couldn't, the trip was going to be very short.

Someone shouted behind them.

Three people rushed out of a side passage. Two of them tackled Rex to the ground.

"Hey!" Rex shouted. "Keep your hands off me!"

He kicked around, but didn't hit anyone. The third person slung a rope over the top of him.

In a flash, Tina produced the gun and pointed it at the men. "Let him go or I'll shoot!"

The three turned to her, bent over Rex.

None of the men were affected by the warty skin condition, but these weren't Federacy troops.

"Back away from him," Tina said, slowly moving forward. She held the weapon outstretched, pointed at each of the men in turn.

"Let him go. Take the rope off his hands." She gestured with the gun.

For a moment, it looked like they were going to obey, but then Rex shouted, "Mum! Behind you!"

Tina whirled around. Saw a fourth man. Fired.

The figure was engulfed in light.

Whirled back around.

One of the three men shouted, "Grab him by the feet. We'll take the other end."

They were after Rex?

Tina held out the gun. "Stay there or you'll join your friend in hell."

The recharge light was still flashing.

Shit. How quickly—or slowly—did this thing recharge?

The men put Rex on his feet, and sheltered behind him.

They walked slowly away from Tina, dragging Rex behind them.

At that moment the lift door opened.

"Tina, what are you...?"

Finn.

One man lifted his hand. The light glinted off a blade of metal.

Tina yelled, "Watch out, he's got a knife!"

Finn ducked the knife. It hit the lift wall behind him with a clang. He dived to pick it up, and flung it back at the thug in a single movement. It hit the man in the neck.

He screamed.

With a snap, Rex broke the rope that held him. He swung his arm, hitting another assailant in the head with such force that he went flying. The man landed with a thud, while the other crumpled to the ground in a pool of blood.

The third man came out from behind Rex, pointing a gun at Finn—Tina fired again.

Rex shouted, "Hey!"

Her shot went past him, hitting the man in the shoulder. He screamed and ran off, clutching his arm and his burning jacket, almost tripping over the gun he dropped. Finn picked up the weapon.

"Mum! What were you doing? You almost shot me!"

"Almost," Tina said.

"Almost is good," Finn said, putting the weapon in his belt.

Rex stared at Tina, open-mouthed. "You freaked me out."

"I liked the snapping of those ropes," Tina said. "But I think you may need some more hero training. Let's go."

Finn picked up one of the bags Rex had dropped and

Rex took the other. The three of them ran through the passage, and Tina was definitely the slowest.

But it didn't take long before footsteps sounded behind them.

Finn glanced over his shoulder.

"How many?" Tina asked.

"Five, six? Too many to shoot."

Shit.

"How ready is the ship?"

"As ready as I could get it. I can't see any faults, but I have no idea how you plan to get out. It's a mess of cables and structures out there. We need to wait for the pilot—"

"No time."

"What? If we try to blunder out by ourselves, we'll take half the docking structure with us."

"So be it. We're getting out."

"But you'll lose docking privileges."

"For escaping from enemy attack? I doubt it."

Tina had no more breath for talking, but while they ran through the passage, she realised the horrible truth. The break-ins had never been about the cactuses. Or maybe only a little bit. What these pirates really wanted was Rex. Her son, who had been born after having been exposed to rift material, and after fifteen years, had not shown any deterioration of his skin or his mind. And she was sure as hell not going to let them get their hands on him.

They got to the ship's docking tube.

Rasa sat in the entrance under her blanket, the geese mildly alarmed at the fast approaching runners.

"Get out of the way!" Tina called.

Rasa got up, clutching her blanket, her eyes wide.

Tina ran into the tube. She registered that the panel next

to the door was on and showed 100% readiness. She pushed open the door. It still stuck, but it was only the inner door, because the airlock was folded outwards for docking. Damn, she hoped it still worked, because she hadn't tested it.

Into the cabin.

She flung off her jacket and gun, hit "prepare for departure" and dropped into the pilot's seat. The outside projectors and the banks of control lights came on.

Rex and Finn also came in.

People outside shouted.

"Hurry up! Shut that door. I'm going to disconnect!" She attached her earpiece, attempting to listen to the control centre over the yelling. "Can you shut up? I need to hear the control centre."

"Mum!"

"What?" Tina turned around, pushing down one half of the earpiece, ready to tell him to sit the hell down and strap in.

But he stood in the aisle, holding a white goose.

Tina stared at him and he stared back.

"She lost her home," Rex said. "If she stays here, she'll be sold off. I'll look after her, I swear."

All kinds of thoughts went through Tina's head. She'd only ordered supplies for three people, not four people and five geese. She didn't want to be responsible for any strays while she didn't even have her own shit sorted out.

But all of that faded into insignificance with Rex's words, *she'll be sold*.

If ever she'd be responsible for one girl being sold off as sex slave, she could never live with herself.

"All right. Strap her in. Try to get those animals locked up somewhere. Shut the airlock. Come and sit here."

Finn went to the door, pulled Rasa inside. She didn't appear to understand what was happening and protested with a squeal. The geese ran through the cabin, honking loudly.

"Get those birds out of my way!" Tina called.

Rex sank into the chair next to her, which he could, because he fit between the control panel and the chair.

Tina pulled out a control console and shoved it at him. "Work out how to disconnect the tube."

She got up again, because Finn was chasing the geese around the cabin. Tina grabbed a safety blanket and chased two of the birds into a corner. She trapped them with the blanket, looped it around the loudly protesting birds and shoved them into the cargo hold. Finn had caught the other two geese while the fifth one was still running around the cabin.

The inner door slid shut.

Rex said, "Are we ready? Disconnecting now."

If the irising air lock still worked.

Tina ran back to her seat and reconnected her earpiece.

No, they weren't ready. Someone needed to strap Rasa in and show her the safety mask. Tina needed to study the way out of this maze.

The airlock mechanism zoomed. Metal clanged and clicked. A hiss of air indicated the sealing of the cabin. The air vents came on.

The *free* light came on. The gravity shifted. A tool belt floated into the middle of the cabin.

A squawk sounded behind her, and a highly panicked goose flew through the cabin. Crashed into the wall. A couple of feathers added to the floating debris.

Rasa called out, and a lot of yelling ensued.

Benny informed her helpfully, "I detect foreign biological material."

Rocket science, that.

The ship was drifting further. They had to get moving or they'd tumble into an uncontrolled path.

Tina tested the engine. It responded, pushing the ship a tiny distance from the station.

But now the navigation refused to come up.

Benny said, "Need to install update before system is operational."

Well, that was helpful.

Finn dropped into the seat to her other side, breathing deeply. "I strapped them in together."

Tina noticed a trickle of blood running down his cheek. "You're bleeding. How good are you at manual navigation?"

"Yes, well…" He wiped his face with his sleeve, smearing the blood all over his cheek. "Not my strongest subject. Have you got a map?"

Tina brought up the display.

Finn blew out a breath. "Shit, it's a tangle out there."

"I told you so. I need a direction pronto because I'm out of contact with the station and we'll start diverging soon."

The station and everything attached to it rotated, and now that the ship was loose, the slightest movement would bring them out of sync.

Finn started reading out sets of coordinates and Tina fed them into the navigation system—that had been recalibrated since Benny had updated.

Tina carefully navigated the ship between two metal struts, but the station already rotated and now that the ship was no longer attached, it had its own momentum.

A voice sounded in her ear. "Kelso Station Control to

unknown pilot. Please return to port. Kelso Station Control to unknown pilot..."

Tina shut it down.

She glanced aside at a small noise next to her.

A goose, standing next to her, looking curiously at the screen.

"What is that bird doing in here?"

"Sorry, they all ended up in the cabin," Finn said. "The door wouldn't stay shut."

Tina looked over her shoulder. Rasa sat strapped in her seat, pale-faced, with the other four geese around her.

"Restrain those animals. We'll soon need to pick up some speed. I don't want them flailing about the cabin."

"Feed them some pellets," Rasa said. "They will come."

She handed a box to Rex, who drifted, shaking the box, to the back of the cabin. The geese half-walked, half-flew after him.

Tina studied the dock's structures, in between little bursts of power from the engine that kept them up to speed with the rotating station. They could move only slowly. Finn warned her of nearby dangers.

A proximity alarm started blaring.

They were too close to another docking tube. The ship that was attached to it was positively ancient, and had been ancient even when it had last been used. The surface was scarred and pitted. Another bulky ship lay on the other side, a walkway below them, and arrays of cables hanging off the exterior hull.

"Straight up," Finn said.

Tina looked. "I don't have much room to turn."

But she made the turn anyway.

In between another walkway and the lift tube was a

narrow gap. The curve of the planet was visible in between all the docking installations.

"That's not going to fit," Tina said.

"Turn ninety degrees."

Tina found a point to fix on to keep the ship's speed the same as the station's rotating speed and then turned the ship on its side.

"Hey!" Rex protested.

"If it bothers you, keep your eyes shut," Tina said.

"I don't feel so good," Rasa said.

"Rex, make sure that if anyone spews, they do it in one of the bags that are in the armrests."

Tina increased the engine power.

The ship moved forward.

But then...

A massive shape blocked the view of the planet through the opening. It was a ship, but not the blocky and functional shape of the SS *Stavanger*.

"What is that thing? It's massive."

Tina killed the process that ramped up the engine, staring at the behemoth coming past.

The grey surface kept coming and coming. Hatches, missile firing turrets, external pipe work.

"It's a pirate ship," Finn said.

"That? I thought pirates operated in small bands."

"They *did*, that's what I've been trying to tell you. They got together. They occupied stations and sectors of space."

The ship still drifted forward through the gap. At this rate, they were going to emerge right into the pirate's ship's view. She didn't know what their shielding would be like, but she had no desire to test it.

They drifted past another opening.

Here, she could see the planet, too, but the view was much less clear, barred by the intricate structure of antennas and wiring of the station's communication array.

Tina hit the power.

Finn gasped. "What are you doing?"

The ship shot forward and then into the opening.

"Hold on!" Tina said.

And the next moment a sharp thwack indicated the first impact.

Tina steered the ship to the side. It missed a main beam but cut a swathe through a forest of small antennas. The proximity alarm blared constantly.

"Mum, what are you doing? You're going to damage the ship."

"This is a pretty tough old boat." Tina pressed her lips together, navigating between the more solid structures as best she could. She turned off the alarms. Better do some minor damage than running foul of that behemoth.

Then they were free.

"That ship's going to come after us?" Rex said.

"No, it's not," Finn said. "Look, that's the SS *Stavanger* getting ready to engage it."

Tina enlarged the view on the main screen and saw he was right. The SS *Stavanger* was moving out of dock as the pirate ship glided into safety by putting the station in between the two ships.

She blew out a breath. "I don't know how that's going to end, but it seems a good place not to be at the moment."

For once, luck was with Tina, and the Federacy Force did what it was meant to do, while Tina pulled away from the station into the darkness of space.

CHAPTER THIRTY-TWO

IT WAS ALL BACKWARDS.

Normally, you did inventories and checks before departure.

Now, Tina needed to do the checks after she was sure they had escaped safely.

The ship had enough fuel but they were a bit short on food for the journey to Olympus with one extra person and a few geese.

Once they were well away from the station, Tina could give the command to unfold the habitat arms and set them into motion so that passengers could move in there and experience a semblance of gravity.

That brought the necessity of a new round of cleaning by Rex and Finn, while she stabilised the ship and checked the autopilot. The level of dust in the habitats was not as high as in the control cabin because they had been stowed for all the time the ship was in dock. The smell, however, was something different altogether.

The geese were not happy in the weightless cargo hold,

so they would have to reserve a cabin in the habitat, and somehow wrestle them down there.

Rasa herself had retreated to the back of the ship. She clung onto the back wall with her blanket, shying away from anyone who came near, especially Finn. Neither Finn nor Rex could convince her to move.

When the autopilot was stable, Tina abandoned the controls and went to her, trying to unloop her arms from her knees, but she hung there, shivering, in a tightly-held ball. The tang of vomit hung around her.

"Come on, it's safe now."

"I don't want to leave anymore," Rasa said.

"It's too late. You're stuck with us, so we might as well make you part of the crew."

"I don't feel well."

"Go down into the habitat. You won't feel so bad there. Do you still want to find your brother?"

Rasa nodded. Her eyes were wide.

"Then come with me."

Tina managed to pry her loose and guided her towards the opening to the passage that led to the habitat. She pulled herself down the passage until the artificial gravity started pulling at her and climbed the rest of the way down the ladder.

Finn and Rex had cleaned up the habitat and, with its comfy couches and warm lighting, it looked much friendlier than the cabin. Currently, the walls displayed a forest, so it looked like a cabin in the woods. Tina gave Rasa one of her shirts and a pair of trousers, which were much too wide, but also found a belt to hold them up.

They'd be unlikely to make it to Olympus in one trip,

and if they stopped somewhere, new clothes for Rasa would be on the shopping list.

Rasa looked a bit more comfortable now. "You said you'd help me find my brother?"

"If we can. What do you know about him?"

She opened a heart-shaped locker she wore around her neck and pulled out a tiny stained card with a picture of a young man. In a Federacy Force uniform. Great.

Tina went in search of the food supplies, sorted them into breakfasts, lunches and dinners. "Just so that you don't think I'll provide all the catering, I'll show you how the food preparation works, so you can do it yourself. I'm going to divide the food up into daily rations, because we'll be short, and I have no idea what's going to be facing us. Do we have any news on Kelso yet, Finn?"

Finn picked up the control module from the table, and changed the display on the walls from showing a tranquil forest to showing Kelso Space Station.

"Whatever is happening, there is no external sign of damage."

"Where are the two ships?"

"Circling each other. See? There's the SS *Stavanger*."

Yes, Tina saw it.

Finn said, "If they're going to play that game, the *Stavanger* has a lot of onboard supplies. I'm sure it can keep going for a year."

"I don't know. Everything about that pirate ship says to me to never underestimate them." Tina could see in Finn's eyes that he knew that. "Looks like you stepped out just in time."

"It's a rotten thing to do to your mates," he said, looking at his hands.

Tina knew that feeling. She also knew that there should be more news about the attack on Kelso, but it was likely that the news was being suppressed by the station authorities under the influence of Jake.

"How many stations do the pirates control?" she asked.

Finn said, "It's a battle for each individual station. We don't always hear the results, especially if the pirates win."

Up until now, Tina hadn't realised how desperate the situation was.

She asked, "What do the pirates want with the stations they've taken?"

"Good question. To control the communication, resupply and docking, I guess."

Tina wondered if cactuses was another reason. But answering that question would be for later.

First they needed to get to Olympus safely.

The first thing was to start training Rex as a full-fledged crewmember. He was still awkward in his new harness, and Tina wanted him to be able to help Finn with tasks that were just so much easier with more than one person, like configuring the ship. He would also need some weapons training and hand-to-hand combat training in case they were boarded or needed to enter another ship or station.

Then she would have to find some way of making Rasa useful.

What they would do when they got to Olympus was a question that would be answered later. For one, no one knew if the world was still solidly in Federacy hands. But if it was possible, Tina would deliver the material she had left in the box fifteen years ago, as well as the letter by Vasily, to the assembly. Then the decision about the next step in fighting the menace would no longer be in her hands.

If it was up to her, she'd try to isolate the pirates and find out how the alien infection spread, and then what to do about it. She would head that project if they asked her, as long as they didn't ask her to re-enlist in the Federacy Force. But a civilian scientific organisation? Totally.

She had no guarantee, though, that the Federacy Assembly would see things her way. If Tina knew one thing, it was that governments worked in strange ways.

———

THE STORY CONTINUES with book 2, Originator, in which Tina and her crew are forced to get supplies on Aurora Station, and find a big surprise waiting for them.

Buy Originator on the author's website, pattyjansen.com

ABOUT THE AUTHOR

Patty Jansen lives in Sydney, Australia, where she spends most of her time writing Science Fiction and Fantasy.

Her story *This Peaceful State of War* placed first in the second quarter of the Writers of the Future contest and was published in their 27th anthology. She has also sold fiction to genre magazines such as Analog Science Fiction and Fact, Redstone SF and Aurealis.

Patty has written over thirty novels in both Science Fiction and Fantasy, including the *Icefire Trilogy* and the *Ambassador* series.

pattyjansen.com

BOOKS BY PATTY JANSEN

MORE INFORMATION:

PATTYJANSEN.COM